Starr's Awakening

Red Starr, The Prequel

Kennedy Layne

STARR'S AWAKENING

Copyright © 2014 by Kennedy Layne
Print Edition
E-Book ISBN: 978-0-9908860-1-3
Print ISBN: 978-0-9908860-2-0

Dedication

Jeffrey—you awakened my heart and soul. I love you.

Cole—high school is your prequel. Enjoy these years and kick off the bright future ahead of you with friends and happiness. I am beyond proud of you.

Chapter One

ATORI STARR STARED at the thunderous waves of the Atlantic Ocean as they rolled onto the white sand only to be sucked back into the vast void. The strong tide gave them no say in the direction they wanted to take. She understood how the untamed foaming caps felt as the massive body of water dictated their efforts. Her fate had been taken out of her hands and there wasn't a thing she could do to change any of it.

Reminiscing over the same memories for the past two years kept *him* alive in her heart. Their wedding night played over and over in Catori's head until yet other special moments crowded in. She had numbed herself to the pain and went through her days in a mindless state doing absolutely nothing. Within the span of a single hour on a critical mission, her life had been ripped to shreds. She hadn't been there in his last few minutes of life and she felt the guilt eat at her soul every second of every hour of every day. The part she couldn't accept was no one survived in whom she could seek solace or revenge. The spirit within her anguished over that fact and constantly pierced her heart as a reminder. There was nothing left.

The evening air contained a chill, which had her pulling the beige crocheted knit sweater that Brendan had bought her on their honeymoon over her shoulders just a little bit tighter. The evening sun was setting, but Catori couldn't bring herself to move from the bench along this stretch of the beach. The reservoir of energy that used to course its way through her veins had been depleted long ago. A movement to the right in her peripheral vision caught her eye, and although her old recognition of tradecraft more or less had become dormant, it still existed.

A man was located around a hundred feet away, strolling through the cooling sand with his hands in his pockets and his face toward the breeze. His brown hair was short but still in need of a cut if she could see the strands moving from here. Gavin Crest. She recognized him immediately and she settled back against the wooden bench, accepting that she'd have to bear his company while he had his say.

Catori studied him while she waited, taking in Crest's Tommy Bahama black button-down shirt and khaki shorts. It was rare she saw him wearing something so casual, but the classic style fit his personality. The brown leather sandals were a nice touch and he still wore those Ray Ban sunglasses from years ago in the desert. They'd been friends for a very long time and she knew what he'd come to see her about. She just didn't think she was ready.

Crest pulled out a folder from behind his back that must have been tucked into his waistband and sat down beside her without a word. The two of them continued to stare out over the ocean and Catori found that the company wasn't the same without her husband. She shifted slightly, trying to rid herself of the chill of loneliness that she'd gotten much too acquainted with lately. It wasn't going anywhere anytime soon.

"How did you find me?"

"You didn't make it that hard," Crest replied, lifting the

blacked out sunglasses until they sat perfectly on top of his head. "Besides, yesterday marked the two year anniversary of Red's death. I figured you'd come back to where the two of you met."

Red. Hearing her husband's nickname caused her to wince and Catori could see that Crest hadn't missed her reaction. Brendan O'Neill. He was as Irish as they came and the complete physical opposite of her mixed Apache and English heritage. Saying his name aloud brought his image alive and it was as if he were standing directly in front of her. His nickname stemmed from his tousled blond hair that contained a hint of fire and that damned flame-red beard, but it was his grey eyes that had captured her attention the first time she'd had the privilege to meet him. The vision faded just as quickly as it appeared.

"And you're here why?" Catori already knew the answer to that question, but she felt compelled to let Crest know he wasn't welcome. "I would have thought you would be too busy with setting up your new agency. Speaking of which…Minneapolis? Really? I heard you only see green grass a couple of times a year."

"That's an exaggeration and you know it." Crest shot her a sideways look that said he wasn't humored by her comment. "Besides, I have family in Minnesota. It was time to go back home."

"We have no home, Crest." Catori didn't want to get into another debate with him in regards to family and friends, so she switched the subject by motioning toward the folder in his hand. "What's in the file?"

"Before we get to that," Crest replied, not giving an inch and stirring an irritation that Red had liked to poke from time to time just for the hell of it, "CSA will open its doors shortly. I cherry-picked my team and have also spent time cultivating relation-ships with numerous agencies that I can rely on in specific situations. You and Red had something that can't be thrown away, Starr. You have the ability to lay out a strategy and develop the detailed plan of attack that is required for a highly trained tactician to lead a team into the most dangerous of hostage rescue missions. You have an innate sense of operations in a way that no one else has that I've ever seen. It's time to get back in the game."

"Red Starr HRT died the day Brendan did." Catori hadn't just lost her husband that fateful day, but the group of five men that made up the hostage rescue team had been like brothers...family. She'd stayed back in the States due to another potential assignment they had both thought warranted attention. She'd left men behind and there wasn't a minute that went by that she let herself forget it. "I'm out."

"Really? Is that what Red would want?"

"Don't," Catori warned, sitting a little straighter on the bench. She brushed away her long black hair as she met the gaze of Crest's green eyes. She hated the sympathy she saw within them, and even though she promised herself she wouldn't go on the defensive the words came out anyway. "Red and I started the team together. It was *ours*. Not mine alone. Don't put that bullshit on me, Crest."

"Bullshit? You're the one that's spewing that shit. You're a retired Master Sergeant of the United States Marine Corps, for fuck's sake. Square your ass away and act like the senior staff non-commissioned officer I know you are. You've had your time to grieve for Red. All those years of training didn't teach you to fold at the first roadblock in your path. Hardships are just leadership opportunities. The missions come first. Red knew that and you know that. So sack up and get your ass back in the game."

"Red died alone, Crest." Catori stated the obvious, not

knowing what else to say. She'd come to Ship Bottom in order to remember a past life that she would never get back. Crest didn't get to land blows and ruin the memories. "Where the hell is your compassion?"

"There's compassion and then there's fucking enabling. I won't enable you, Marine," Crest stated, shaking his head to emphasize his words. "We've maintained a friendship over the years and I won't abandon you to lie in your own crap. Face facts. You were always the brains of the outfit. Red was the brawn, an operator. And to be honest with you, it's a lot harder to replace you than it would be him. Find yourself a new lead operator and get back to doing your damn job."

Catori didn't reply, mostly because she had nothing to come back with. Yes, she'd been wallowing in her own misery. Wasn't she entitled to? She'd lost her husband, her partner, her lover. The world had lost a good man, an honest man. The anguish once again hit her chest and she blinked rapidly to contest the tears that she didn't want to appear. It could be going on ten years and she would still feel the same. She'd tried everything imaginable to let go and even resorted to taking a man into her bed last night. It didn't work, which was why she was out here by herself, trying to make sense of what her meaningless days had become. Life wasn't fucking fair and here Crest was, reminding her of that fact.

"It's time, Catori." Crest placed the manila folder between them on the weather worn bench that had lost its color long ago from the harsh elements. She knew how the wood felt, for that's how her soul would appear in the light of day. "There are dossiers inside this file that will give you detailed information on men and women that I've selected for your new team. Take it or leave it, but know that I would hire any one of them for CSA. I've done the grunt work for you—now all you have to do is get your ass back into mission ready status."

Catori didn't reach for the packet or reply to Crest's little speech. She hated that he was right and that she needed to start doing something with her life other than fade away into nothing. Red wasn't here. He was never going to be and it was time that she faced facts, regardless that her heart would never beat the same. It was now hollow and only involuntarily doing what her body asked. If there was anything left to give, it might as well be to those people who needed help. Maybe it would speed up the time that had slowed down to an unbearable crawl, aging her beyond her years. She looked forward to the moment when she and Red would meet again.

Crest stood, not bothering to place his sunglasses back onto his face. Dusk had fallen and the ocean was turning dark, much like the abyss she knew it to be. There was nothing left to be said, but when her friend took two steps away, she found she didn't want to be left alone…not yet.

"What am I going to owe you for taking the time to vet these potential team members?" Catori released the tight hold she had on her sweater and let her fingers brush the folder. She wouldn't admit to the small spark inside of her at doing something slightly different than her monotonous routine of waking up in the morning. This was just to pass the time. "You know I hate favors."

"You owe me nothing more than you did before," Crest replied, stopping but not fully facing her. He turned slightly and looked over his shoulder, hands back into his pockets. "I'm repaying a debt that I owed Red from a long time ago. Take advantage of it, and when you're in my neighborhood give me a call. I'll take you out to dinner, Top"

Catori laughed softly, the sound foreign to her own ears. She watched as Crest walked away, and although he'd said things she hadn't wanted to hear, knew that she had a true friend in that enigmatic man. She and Red had known him for years, but there was something about Gavin Crest that would always remain a mystery. Regardless, she knew whom to call if she were ever in some serious shit.

"Crest," Catori called out, waiting for him to turn around once more. He was at least forty yards out, but she could still make out his form. "You're more likely to be in California than I am in your bitter-assed state. Look me up."

A flash of smile in the early moonlight and then her friend was gone. Catori sat there for a few more moments, wondering why Crest had chosen now of all times to tempt her with something new. He was very much like Red in his timing, but then that's what had made Red so good at his job. She looked down at the file, and giving in, picked it up. She'd wait for morning before seeing what was inside. It felt odd to have something to do besides wake up tomorrow. Waves were still crashing against the sand, fighting against the eternal tide. She knew that's what it would feel like starting over, but maybe this time she could manage to bring them all home.

Chapter Two

C ATORI HELD THE folder underneath her arm as she walked up the porch stairs to the small beach house she and Red had always rented when they visited Ship Bottom. Well, the house *she* now rented the same week, the same month every year. Regardless if she chose to go forward with what Crest was suggesting, she would keep on doing so until her dying breath. Using her key, she opened the door with a little more force than necessary and stepped inside the cool air-conditioned living room, leaving behind the warm evening humidity. The lamp beside the couch had been turned on, lighting up the homey yet tattered furniture. It was quiet and though it sounded as if no one was inside, she felt another's presence and knew yesterday's company remained.

"I didn't think you were coming back."

Catori turned upon hearing Josh's voice coming from the direction of the kitchen. Sure enough, the man she'd picked up at a bar last night stood in the doorframe wearing nothing more than a pair of cut-off denim jean shorts. One muscled arm was leaning against the wooden jamb while he held a bottle of water with his other hand. She suddenly felt a twinge of guilt at picking up a man at least twenty years her junior. It was his disheveled blond hair that had grabbed her attention, looking so close to that of Red's, along with his build. The only thing missing were her husband's red highlights.

"I needed some time to myself. You didn't need to stay."

"That's what I figured," Josh replied in a soft tone, relaying that he didn't have any hard feelings. "For some reason, I couldn't leave without making sure."

Catori placed her keys on top of the folder and set both items on the side table, next to a glass vase with various shells that had been collected from the beach. She wasn't used to being in this predicament; however she found that a part of her was glad Josh had stayed. Discussing the past with Crest had shifted something inside of her and she didn't want to be alone—not yet.

"Do you have to go or can you stay for another hour?" Catori asked, closing the door behind her and then leaning up against the weathered wood. When she and Red had first started out, they hadn't had a lot of money. This was the only place that would give them a decent rate and they'd stayed loyal to the owners. Why she would choose now to bring a man here she didn't know. A psychologist would have a field day with her psyche, but one wasn't here and Josh was. "And just to clarify, it would only be for an hour."

Josh wasn't the type to take offense at what she was offering. He probably had his own reasons for being here, and most likely he did this a lot more often than she did. They were both consenting adults regardless of the fact that she was a hell of a lot older than him. It didn't matter. It was just a physical thing and they both wanted it.

"Yeah, I have an hour." For a brief second, Catori thought she saw a glimmer of sympathy in his eyes and her stomach clenched. She refused to be anyone's pity fuck, and if that's how

Josh saw her he was sorely mistaken. Before she could respond either verbally or physically, he'd already tossed his bottle of water onto the old plaid couch and had her up against the door. She soaked up his virility and ignored everything else. It wasn't like tomorrow wouldn't bring back all the unwanted solitude. "Same rules apply?"

"Yes," Catori whispered, turning her head to the side and offering her neck. She knew it was senseless, but she couldn't find it in her to kiss another man. Sex was sex, nothing more than two people satisfying a basic desire. Kissing was an intimate expression of love and one that she refused to share with anyone other than Red. She couldn't give that up to any other man. "The same rules apply."

Josh's soft lips brushed against Catori's damp skin, the humidity high even with the AC in the drafty old home. She loved the sensation that his moist tongue added to her senses as it traveled to the curve in her neck. Shivers went through her and awakened what had been asleep for so long. He glided his hands underneath her sweater, causing goose bumps that followed the trail of his cool fingers. He let the material slide from her shoulders and onto the ground. She closed her eyes and pushed all thought out of her mind. She wouldn't think of Red or she would ruin it.

"Rougher," Catori murmured, leaning down and sinking her teeth into his bicep. His skin was taut and it felt so nice to have something to bite into, surrendering to her basic urges. Josh had rested his right arm onto the door and his large muscle had been an easy target. She inhaled his scent, loving the fresh ocean fragrance that seemed to adhere to his skin. She ran her tongue over the indentions and only afterward turned her head to meet his sensual green eyes. "You know how I like it after last night."

Josh didn't hesitate as he leaned down and hoisted her legs

over his waist. She was wearing cut-off denim shorts as well, probably a little shorter than was appropriate for her age. She wore them out of necessity for the heat and no other reason. She didn't care what people thought of her body, although she kept herself in excellent shape. She knew her figure was too muscular for some, but being a Marine had taught her to keep healthy and stay fit more out of habit. It was a hard pattern to break. Josh didn't seem to mind her physique if the bulge in his jean shorts was any indication.

Keeping his hands underneath her ass, Josh walked both of them over to the couch and sat down. She straddled him with her legs, placing her knees on either side of him. Seeing as her sweater lay on the floor by the door, the only thing left on her upper body was her faded gray T-shirt, which sported the Marines' motto of Semper Fi in cracked black lettering. She quickly drew it over her head, freeing her congenitally bronzed breasts. She detested bras, and whenever she could get away without wearing one she did. Red preferred...she threw him out of her thoughts.

The palms of Josh's hands circled her ample flesh, roughly massaging her globes and causing her copper nipples to harden. Catori soaked in the physical pleasure of his callused fingers. The way she was sitting on his lap, all he had to do was lean forward to take the darkened flesh into his mouth. The searing heat caused her head to lie back against her shoulders. When his bright white teeth bit down on the sensitive nub she cried out at the sheer intense pleasure.

"Yes," Catori hissed, sliding her fingers through his hair and holding tight. She cradled him closer, wanting to feel some-thing...anything other than what had been consuming her. "More."

Josh pushed her off of him, tackling the button and zipper

on her denim shorts. When they fell to her ankles along with her panties from his prying fingers' insistence, he followed suit with his shorts and slid off of the couch and onto the floor. He made sure he was situated between her legs. A foot on either side of his thighs allowed him entry to her molten core.

Catori once again sank her fingers into his hair and held tight as his mouth sealed over her clit. A severe wave of pleasure washed over her and she had to lock her knees in place so that she didn't collapse as she thrust herself against his mouth. His tongue swirled around her clitoris and flicked lightly, causing her arousal to spike even higher. She needed more and increased her grip on his hair, telling him so.

Josh ran his hands none too gently up her legs, leaving a tingling sensation in his wake. He cupped her ass cheeks and pulled her tighter to him, his tongue pressing harder on her swelling nub. Finally he brought his arm back around the front of her and using what she thought was his middle finger, slid it between her wet folds. His touch was too soft for what she needed.

"More," Catori muttered, surging herself against his mouth. He added an additional finger to her core and forcefully stroked both of them inside of her, massaging her g-spot. It felt so good, that when he did it again, she encouraged him further. "Harder."

Over and over, Josh thrust his arched fingers into her pussy until she was on the brink of an orgasm. The wet sounds of sex bounced off of the walls, the only noise entering through the roar of blood in her ears. He was now sucking on her clit, adding to the stimuli and keeping her hanging on the edge of that precipice. Reality was finally fading away as she concentrated on the pleasure her body was receiving. This was like a shot of adrenaline and she couldn't get enough of it.

Josh stopped what he was doing, much to her annoyance,

but it was to shed his straining briefs and take out a condom from the back pocket of his discarded shorts. Not wanting to delay their satisfaction any longer than was necessary, Catori rose to stand over him while he rolled on the latex. He'd situated himself once more with his back to the couch. The second he was protected, she took over and settled a knee on either side of him. He immediately tried to kiss her, but she pulled her head back just in time. She then grabbed the back of his head and pressed his face against her neck, needing some form of contact but just not the kind he wanted.

Catori reached between them with her other hand and held his cock so that she could sink down and take what she wanted. The fullness created was overwhelming and she held still so she could savor the feeling. When his hands reached between them, catching each nipple in between his thumb and finger, she relished at the slight sting. It felt so fucking good.

"That's it," Catori muttered, urging him on. The pain compelled her further and she used her knees to lift up. Her movement caused his cock to be pulled from her pussy, but she slammed back down onto him for the extra pressure. Pleasure engulfed her, spurring her into action. "Fuck."

Josh didn't let go of her nipples, but instead started rolling and pulling on them, giving her exactly what she needed. She continued to take him inside of her, almost a little too brutally, but it felt too damn good to stop. Her clit was striking his pubic bone with each collision, driving her back into that abyss she craved. The softness of his tongue on her neck was in direct contrast of every other awareness and muddled up her senses.

Catori slammed onto him over and over, holding onto his shoulders for leverage and greedily taking the gratification that he was giving her. It wasn't like he wasn't receiving any himself; therefore it was the perfect exchange. When his cock swelled, indicating his impending release, it triggered something inside of her. She dug her fingers into his solid muscles while she followed him over. The physical satisfaction tore through her, but unfortunately left her hollow on the inside. She rested her forehead against his right shoulder, attempting to catch her breath. He stroked her back, and although he had to know what was coming he didn't make it awkward.

"Thank you," Josh murmured, tenderly kissing her temple. It was so opposite of what they'd just participated in that Catori found his gentleness hard to endure. It did give her the energy to pull away. She lifted herself off of him as gracefully as she could, snatching up her shirt that was lying on the couch. His deep voice caught her off guard. "Here."

Josh was holding up her panties with a small smile, indicating he knew when he'd overstayed his welcome. Catori felt herself softening toward his young charming grin and did her best to return it. She slipped on her Fox and Rose black silk French cut panties, covering herself. Widening the neck of her T-shirt, she drew it over her head while capturing her long black hair, pulling it from underneath the fabric.

"I'm leaving tomorrow afternoon," Catori stated, feeling the need to spell things out. She didn't even know his last name, not that she wanted to. It was easier this way. No mess. "I appreciated the...company."

"The feeling is mutual," Josh said, his soft laughter filling the air as he stood up, oblivious to his naked stature and started to put on his clothes. Catori would have been made of stone not to appreciate his muscular body and the way his skin contained a healthy golden hue that was recognizably from the sun and not his heritage. She realized that his shirt must have been left in the bedroom and she quickly retrieved it. He must have taken care of the condom because by the time she got back to the living room he was standing there waiting for her. He took the shirt from her hands, his fingers purposefully brushing against hers. "If you're ever back in town, you can usually find me at Joe Pop's Shore Bar."

Catori had met Josh at the lively nightspot, so it didn't come as a surprise that he was a regular. She didn't bother asking what he did for a living. More than likely she wouldn't see him again after tonight. It was highly doubtful that he would be here, seeing as he didn't strike her as the type to stay in one place for too long. Once he was dressed, he gave another charismatic smile while waiting on a cue from her.

"I'll keep that in mind," Catori replied, leading the way to the door. She pulled on the knob and kept her hand on it, leaning her head against the edge of the wood as she watched him walk out onto the porch. "Josh?"

He didn't turn around until he'd sprinted down the three battered greying steps. When he did, his appearance in the moonlight seemed younger than what he was, striking a chord in her heart. Josh had the world waiting on him and she wished him nothing but the best. Wanting to say more to him but knowing that would only delay the inevitable, she said the only two words that meant anything.

"Thank you."

Chapter Three

"NO, CATORI... THANK you."

Catori didn't stay where she was to watch Josh leave. Instead she closed the door and then once again leaned her head back onto the hard surface of the allegorical exit. Nothing that had taken place in the last hour, or last night even, had changed her or given her the peace of mind she thought she'd get. In fact, having meaningless sex with someone as sweet and young as Josh had left her feeling somewhat dejected. Pushing herself off what they referred to in the Corps as the *Endex*, she threw the deadbolt, not that it would keep anyone out if they were determined to get in. What she needed was a hot shower, hoping like hell it washed away this pitiful solitude.

Catori made her way through the living room and into the small bedroom. The older furniture in here wasn't any better than what was throughout the house. A mattress with sheets, one bedside table, and a dresser consisted of the boudoir, but considering she'd slept on a fold out canvas cot most of her time in the field, she wouldn't complain. Plus, this house held a place in her heart that no five-star hotel could ever take.

Catori spun the knob for the water, doing her best not to mull over the fact that she'd just brought a man into a special place that had been only hers and Red's. She peeled off her clothes and waited for the water to steam before stepping underneath the plentiful lines of water. She faced the showerhead, letting the hot beads rain down over her body. She hadn't stopped to think that bringing Josh here would sully her memories with Red. She'd just wanted to feel something, anything other than this tortured seclusion she'd done to herself.

Tears were now mixing with the water and Catori was unable to stop them. She would have thought that she had no more, but the grief would always hit her out of nowhere and produce more. She didn't want more, but whenever she tried to prevent them they continued in droves. Now was no different. She'd ruined their special place. What would Red think of that? Whether on purpose or without thought, she'd sullied their memories and she would never get them back.

Catori leaned on the shower wall as the reality of what she'd done sank in, lowering herself to the floor as sob after sob wracked her body. She placed her arms around her legs and rested her forehead on top of her knees as she tried to breathe. Why did he leave her? Why didn't he fight harder to stay alive? Why hadn't she been there to save him or at least be taken with him? This was the worst punishment imaginable, being left alone with no one to share her pain. There wasn't a day that passed that she hadn't wondered what she'd done to deserve this sentence of loneliness. She'd never again feel his hands on her body. She'd never get to taste his lips or hear him sing in the shower. She'd been abandoned.

The ill-fated phone call echoed through Catori's mind as if it were happening now. The words saying that Red and the team hadn't checked in at the designated time had been a blow, but she'd never once considered they'd been killed. She would have felt it—an icy claw around her heart. Once the twelve-hour mark had passed and then the twenty-four hour check had come and gone, she'd reached out to some officials she'd had contact with at the State Department. She'd scrambled for days to figure out a way into the hostile territory, but some kind of incident had provoked the combatants. Thinking she'd be better off to use whatever resources she'd had through Red Starr HRT's contacts, it wasn't until later that she'd realized going in herself would have provided her more answers.

No survivors. Fire had been exchanged, along with grenades, mortars, and artillery. The village had been burned to the ground. Decimated. Nothing of value was left, so the bodies had been thrown into a mass grave, burned and then what remained had been buried. These phrases were said over and over until Catori had thrown up the contents of her stomach. She hadn't known one could get physically ill over grief, but she'd experienced it firsthand. She went into denial for the longest time, using every resource available for more confirmation. Nothing. Absolutely nothing.

"Why, Red?" Catori whispered hoarsely, leaning her head back against the ceramic tile. "Why would you leave me here alone?"

She knew it was unfair of her to ask such a question. It wasn't like he'd had a choice and it sure as hell wasn't like he was going to answer. Her chest hurt from the pain and there wasn't a single moment that went by when it wasn't there. She'd learned to live with it but would have given anything to have it go away. The only person who could do that was Red and he wasn't here anymore. He would never be here. He wasn't ever coming back.

Had he thought of her in those last few moments? Had he called out her name? The one uncertainty that constantly whirled around in her mind was if he'd suffered. How long had it been before he'd stopped breathing, thus ending his suffering? The questions never stopped and they haunted her every night, triggering nightmares of artillery strikes that were beyond her conception.

Catori wasn't sure how long she'd been sitting in the ceramic tub of the shower, but the chill of the water finally registered. She rose to her knees and grappled with the handle, trying to turn it off. She used the knob to help her stand and tried to wipe away the tears. Shivering and trying to stop her teeth from chattering, she opened the shower door and saw the pitiful reflection of herself in the mirror.

Catori didn't know the woman who stared back at her. Her Native American heritage was evident in her long black hair, bronze skin, and dark brown, almost black eyes. She now resembled an apparition of who she once was. Her hair was nowhere near the vibrant shiny black it was in its natural state. It hung in strands as if she were deathly sick. The skin under her eyes looked haunted and her cheeks had become gaunt. As for her eyes, there was no soul present—black as a pit. It had departed this earth the moment she'd heard her husband had left her alone.

Not bothering with a towel, knowing there was no warmth to be had there, Catori exited the bathroom and walked across the room. She opened a window to allow some of the humidity inside and could just make out the sound of the waves as they continued to crash onto the sand. She was glad she hadn't turned on a light in the bedroom as she made her way to the bed. She curled up in the middle of the mattress, hugging one of the pillows tight against her chest.

Catori knew she couldn't go on like this. She'd come to the realization that bringing another man here might have been her way of letting go. Subconsciously, that was. She'd been lost for so long that she wasn't sure of anything anymore. Exhaustion settled over her, but sleep was elusive as usual. No matter how many times the plaguing questions came to the forefront there were never any solutions.

As Catori's muscles finally loosened enough and her chills subsided, her thoughts finally drifted to the folder that was sitting in the living room. Did she have it in her to start over? As physically exhausted as she was now, she wasn't certain if she was up to the task. If she took that step she would have to be intimately involved with each and every hostage rescue mission that took place. Never again would she put herself in the position of hearing through back channels or secondary comms that her team hadn't made it out—that her husband wasn't coming home.

Catori stared out through the sheer curtains, catching glimpses of the moonlight as the clouds rolled through underneath. Had today's events been a sign? Was Red somewhere out there looking out for her, knowing she'd reached her limit? Again, questions that would forever remain unanswered. She promised herself that come morning she would look at the dossiers that Crest had put together for her. Whether or not she carried through with the task ahead was another matter altogether. One thing was for certain...if she were to direct another team, she would never change the name. Red Starr HRT would always and forever carry the title of her husband, for he would always remain *yah-ik-tee*.

Chapter Four

PICKING UP HER travel mug of coffee and Crest's folder, Catori slipped on her oversized sunglasses and headed for the beach. The weather was still on the chilly side so she wore her favorite crocheted sweater once again, although this time she had on a pair of sweats. That still didn't mean she would be parted from her flip-flops. The only way that was happening was if she had on her military issued combat boots that she used to wear on assignment. It made her wonder where they were and figured they were back home in California. It was still up in the air whether or not she'd pull them out and dust them off.

Her hair was drawn back into a ponytail, and with the glasses covering up the bags underneath her eyes, Catori figured she looked younger if the stares she was receiving from a group of twenty-something men playing volleyball were anything to go by. Mentally shrugging off their attention, she made her way a good fifty yards away to her favorite bench spot and took a seat, grateful that no one else seemed to be around this early in the morning.

Catori laid the file next to her and stared out over the ocean. Seagulls were making dives into the water, trying to catch their breakfast while the white caps of the waves still struggled to

make their way higher up onto the sand. She watched a large
sailboat miles out as it made its way across the horizontal
daybreak. Taking a sip of her coffee, she also tasted the salt on
her lips from the sea spray.

A jogger passed by with earbud cords hanging from his head.
His pounding footsteps could be heard from yards away and she
fought the urge to tell him that he was doing it wrong. Instead,
she drank more of her coffee and realized that she actually tasted
the flavor this morning. She turned her head, catching sight of
the jogger as he kept running down the beach. His form was
incorrect, and before too long she knew that his back would
start to hurt within a mile. She hadn't stopped using her
workouts to relieve stress, but she'd been afraid to do her daily
run in the morning for fear she would keep going and never
come back. The itch to resume again was just under the
surface—that lingering taste for the endorphins she craved.

Taking a deep breath, Catori didn't know whether to be
happy or sad that some of those long ago, everyday urges were
returning. Instead of feeling either, she closed her eyes and
raised her face toward the early morning sun and soaked up what
warmth it was providing. It was still early spring and Mother
Nature seemed to be having trouble acclimating. She knew
exactly what she was experiencing.

Catori wasn't sure if she sat on the bench enjoying the early
morning peace for one minute or one hour, but either way her
coffee was now cool. Putting it aside, she finally picked up the
dossiers and placed them on her lap. She traced the outer edge
with her finger, wondering what waited on her inside this file.
Crest wouldn't have picked anyone but the best, yet she already
knew before looking inside at their resumes that she would
nitpick their credentials all the way down to the way they tied
their damn boots. She quickly pulled back the front cover of the

manila folder before she could change her mind.

Hours later, Catori shuffled the papers back in order and placed them inside the folder. Eight names, five slots. The more she read about them the pickier she became. Three men were a given—Kane Taylor, Aaron Scott, and Daegan Murphy. The other two slots would have to be chosen upon a personal meeting. That wasn't to say that she wouldn't catch the other three in their personal environment. The thought brought her up short. Did that mean she was going to go through with this? Did that mean Red Starr HRT would once again be open for business?

The missions would never be the same. Catori wouldn't have Red to bounce ideas off of or tell her that she was being too conventional. He had always told her that she had trouble thinking outside the box, which was why they had made such good partners. He'd been the risk taker as an elite operator and she had been the one with common sense as an operational planner and logistics specialist. Red had teased her endlessly over that and he would be the first to ask her where her good judgment had gone. She wanted to wail at him that had she been with him on that last mission it might not have gone so terribly wrong. *What ifs* could drive a person to a brutal end.

As if Red were sitting next to her and urging her on, she thought through everything that would be needed to resurrect Red Starr HRT. The camaraderie would be different and Catori would need to spend time with the men, training them to Red's specifications. Crest was right when he said that Brendan had been the brawn. She'd need a lead operator, an Alpha male that led from the front, although one who knew his place. He would need to be an apex predator that could take orders and yet exercise initiative when needed. The success of this endeavor would, in large part, rest in whom she selected in this role—if in fact she even followed through with it at all. She would be the one to make any ultimate decisions. The edges of the thick file dug into Catori's skin as she held it tight with her fingers, oscillating in her decision. Was she ready? Could she do this by herself?

A large raven flapped his wings as he softly landed on the back of the bench, joining Catori in her indecision. She looked over at the black-feathered bird, usually in search of prey. Was he as tired as she was? Did he need a break, like the two years she'd given herself? She'd been taught at an early age not to miss the signs that were being gifted. A raven here on the beach was somewhat unusual this far down the East Coast, but she could hardly miss the gravity of his arrival. For many tribes the raven was seen as a trickster because of his ability to shape change; however, holy men of many tribes called upon the raven to clarify their visions. He was a symbol of metamorphosis and change—a great harbinger of transformation. As if knowing he'd done his job, the raven cocked his head toward her and then flew away, signifying it was time for her to find her wings.

Chapter Five

Two months later...

CATORI SWUNG HER red BMW Alpine Z8 convertible into a slot of a practically vacant parking lot of a rundown building posing as a garage. The faded and chipped cinder blocks that kept the square construction standing looked like it could be blown down with one small gust of wind. Summer had finally arrived, although a person wouldn't know it by coming to this place. All the doors were shut along with the two paint-peeling garage doors. It wasn't the most welcoming sight, but from what she'd seen of Mississippi she wasn't surprised.

She'd spent the past eight weeks back home in California, making calls to reestablish old contacts. It wasn't as hard to do as Catori thought it was going to be and she managed to revive over eighty-percent of her prior operational and logistics connections. The initial weapons she'd spent the last week acquiring had cost a pretty penny. In order to obtain the remaining weapons she would acquire she needed to install an appropriate armory to house them with twenty-four hour monitored security.

She hadn't touched the money in Red Starr HRT's bank accounts, and the fact that she still held a Class 3 Federal

Firearms License eased the pain of getting what they needed. She'd contacted the storage unit holding most of the technology equipment she'd packed away and had everything delivered to her new base of operations—a bonded warehouse located on the southwest edge of the Unified Port of San Diego near Chula Vista. It had taken two weeks alone to figure out what needed upgrading and what could be salvaged.

The new building and grounds provided enough room for their brand new Sikorsky MH-60S Knighthawk, a medium lift helicopter, to have a new landing pad when they didn't have it aboard the *Promised Land*.

The *Promised Land* was once a one thousand four hundred fifty ton three hundred six foot converted Crosley-Class High Speed Transport, or APD. She was currently moored along the pier outside the new Red Starr HRT facility. Sold for scrap in the mid-seventies, the ship had been used by numerous enterprises until Red had acquired it nearly twelve years ago. Since its return from Red's last ill-fated mission, Catori had left it setting in dry dock awaiting a refit that Red had taken years to design. The crew had just finished the last minute shakedown cruise and was working on a very long list of red lines.

Considering the new Knighthawk hadn't been delivered in time for the shakedown, Catori was certain the red line list would grow. All of Red Starr HRT's assets were now either being actively moved to the new base in San Diego or being dispositioned. She'd hired an entire team of support personnel, however, she hadn't technically hired one team member that was required to complete the organization's primary mission. That was about to change.

Catori pushed up her sunglasses so they rested on top of her head, taking time to study the layout. John "Trigger" Dixon was third up on her list and was supposedly employed at Mac's Auto

Repair, the dilapidation in front of her. Recalling Trigger's dossier, she didn't find that surprising. He liked working with his hands and this would give him the outlet he needed after serving his time in the service. She was working her way backwards on the list and would save her lead operator for last. The first two men she met weren't the right fit, although that didn't mean they weren't good at what they did. Red had always claimed she was too selective.

Opening the car door, Catori swung her denim-clad legs out of the vehicle and placed her sensible knee-high flat boots onto the graveled dirt. Much to her dismay, she'd ended up having to wear something else besides flip-flops and her issued boots. Knowing she should be presentable, she still chose something comfortable. Her black form-fitting blazer contained a thin belt, which she straightened before slamming her car door. The way the bottom of her coat flared over her waist it was easy to carry her Sig Sauer 9mm M11-A1 in a RHS Paddle holster on her right hip.

The only sounds to carry through the air were the rocks shifting under her weight and a bird cawing on a power line. The place seemed uninhabited, yet the bubbly blonde waitress at the diner in town said that Trigger would be here.

Walking to the tattered painted black door where the top window contained a diagonal crack within its structure, Catori tried the handle but found it locked. She rapped on the glass. When no one appeared, she wiped off the grime of dirt on the pane with her fist. Inside looked deserted, with a cluttered office directly in front of her and an empty stall to her right. The one farther down contained a heap of metal and she wasn't so sure what the make and model was. Shit, she wasn't sure it *could* be restored.

Taking a step back, Catori looked to her left and then to her right. She glanced back over her shoulder toward the long stretch of road and saw the oils of the blacktop surface rising as it baked in the sun. It was boiling out here and she wanted this meeting finalized so she could complete her drive to Missouri by nightfall. Deciding to go around back, she was walking along the side of the garage when she heard a growl that stopped her in her tracks.

"Good boy," Catori said in a soothing tone in hopes that the large German Shepherd remained calm. The beautiful animal was standing toward the back of the building, his brown eyes riveted to her. She stayed where she was, not wanting to give the dog any reason to attack. "I'm friendly, Shep. No threat here."

"Diesel, down." The deep raspy voice that had given the order belonged to a man with a lean muscular form, not quite six feet tall. He wore a baseball cap twisted on backwards and he was wiping grease from his hands with an oil rag. His black shaggy hair immediately gave away that this was the man she was looking for. "Can I help you, ma'am?"

"You can if you're John 'Trigger' Dixon."

Catori waited for the Shepherd to sit back on his hunches. She didn't comment on the dog's name, however apropos it might be considering he guarded a mechanic's garage. From what her research suggested, Dixon worked for Mac. The older man was on the verge of retirement and he'd given a job to John upon arriving back home from his deployment. The former military man had to be ready to pull his hair out, no matter how striking it might be.

"Trigger?" John casually looked down at her waist where her weapon rested before going back to removing the grease from his fingers. "You're military. I think you've come to the wrong place. I've done my duty to my country, ma'am. With the amount of metal in my left arm, I'm not really needed anymore."

"I would disagree with that statement." Catori could see the interest in his brown eyes, so she continued with her inquiry. There was something in his demeanor that struck a chord with her. Chemistry was vital when working with others in a life and death situation. She liked this man. "Your close combat maneuvers are outstanding. That kind of talent shouldn't be wasted."

"It's not a skill that's often used in the civilian world." Trigger stuck his rag in his back pocket before crossing his arms and leaning up against the cinder blocks. She was happy to see that she had his attention. "You want to cut to the chase?"

"I like a man who's direct. As much as I'd like to sum this up within three words and be on my way, it's not that simple." Catori nodded toward the building. "Mind if we go inside where the sun won't bake us both to death?"

"This?" Trigger said with a laugh, looking up toward the sky. "This ain't nothin'."

That Southern charm and the offhanded comments of his would come in handy, especially if the team were engaged in an intimate conflict. This type of carefree attitude could sometimes defuse a hostile situation. Then again it could also be used in a wrong manner, leading to disarray. It was Catori's place to make the call if he knew how and when to talk himself out of precarious situations.

"If it's all the same to you, I'd rather not go over my proposition outside in the heat." Catori studied him and caught the interest he had in her statement. Crest had added a personal note on Trigger's profile stating that he was a professional at maintaining his cool in hostage situations, having proven himself time and again within a Special Operations Unit within the Marines. He was a thirty-one year old man and his calm demeanor was something she wanted for the team. "I think you'll want to hear what I have to say."

Trigger considered her offer, showing the patience that had been instilled within him from childhood. His background stated that his parents were still married and lived in the same house that they had raised their family in. His father was a manager of the local bank while Trigger's mother had stayed at home to take care of her children. Dixon's sister was married with two school-aged children and lived in the same neighborhood where she was raised. It was an all American family that had written to Trigger regularly and had always been there to greet him upon arriving back into the States. When he nodded, she knew that she'd garnered his attention enough to hear the rest of what she had to say.

Catori warily looked at the dog as she took a step forward, but Diesel seemed unaffected now that Trigger had given him a command. Diesel was Mac's dog, from what the waitress had said at the diner. He shouldn't be a problem going forward. She'd seen K-9s do wonderful things out in the field, but there wasn't a place for him on her team. She would have sworn she heard laughter in the light breeze that suddenly kicked up, causing the dust at her feet to rise as she continued to follow Trigger around the back of the building.

"Can I offer you something to drink?" Trigger asked, motioning toward an old vending machine that had just as much grime on it as everything else in the garage. She honestly didn't care about the dirt, having slept some nights in places people wouldn't walk in during the daytime. If he thought this place would make her uncomfortable, she was looking forward to proving him wrong. Unfortunately there wasn't any air conditioning, but at least they were out of the sun. "I think the expiration dates are still good on those cans."

"No, thank you." Catori smirked and shook her head, indicating that she was fine for now. They continued to the front where she'd seen the disorganized office, which did strike a nerve. Her work place was clean, efficient, and damn well organized. No wonder this place wasn't a booming business. It didn't even look like Mac owned a computer. "May I?"

Catori gestured toward the only guest chair, with its torn leather and rusted metal back. Trigger swiped a magazine off of the surface and continued around the desk until he took up residence in the larger rolling chair that had definitely seen better days. Once they were seated, he looked pointedly at her. It was clear that he felt he didn't need to start the conversation.

"I'll make this simple. Your skill as a close combat operator is required to round out my team. I'm offering you a position on a hostage rescue squad that will be taking cases the FBI and others won't touch. This includes domestic as well as assignments abroad. Some won't be pretty and you might want to make sure your personal affairs are up-to-date. For each mission completed, a healthy check will be placed into your account. An additional stipend will be paid during any down time as a retainer and training is provided for all mission-essential tasks at my cost. Life insurance and medical benefits will be provided and the amount you receive in salary will more than cover your additional expenses for living in the greater San Diego area."

Silence descended over the small office with the exception of a ticking clock on the oily wall. The paint looked like it was peeling off, but Catori thought maybe it was just the way stains of smoke lay on the surface. Mac must be a chain smoker from the way the rust colored streaks lined the walls. She waited for Trigger to say something, appreciating that he was taking his time before making a life-altering decision.

"Who are you?"

Catori had been waiting for that question, actually dreading it. Trigger had asked so quietly, she wasn't so sure she hadn't made it up in her head. Within the small community of elite operators, everyone had known Red. She wasn't worried that Trigger would say no to her offer. She was more concerned that he would accept it based on Red's legacy. She wasn't her husband and would never trade on his name.

"Catori Starr—retired Marine Master Sergeant. You can call me Starr."

"Shit, you're Brendan O'Neill's wife. Red Starr HRT." Trigger sat a little straighter in the chair and rubbed his chin, leaving a small streak of black oil in his wake. His statement confirmed her suspicions. This felt like déjà vu, considering she'd just had this conversation over the last three days with two other men. There were many more to go. His brown eyes softened in compassion. "I'm sorry for your loss. I heard that he had been killed overseas. I had the honor of meeting him once, years ago."

"Gavin Crest seems to think you'd make an excellent addition to Red Starr HRT," Catori replied, ignoring his condolences. She glanced at her watch and signaled she wanted this meeting to conclude. Honestly, she'd made up her mind the moment he'd ordered Diesel down. There was a quality of inner strength to his voice that couldn't be taught. He'd been born to be a leader and he was wasting his talents here, although she was sure Mac would dispute that fact. "I agree with Crest. You're well qualified and your last mission provided me with the information I need to know. You'll find additional details to the position that I'm offering you in your email. I'd like a binding answer within the next forty-eight hours. You can sign the detailed offer letter and fax it back or you can just let the deadline expire."

Catori stood and reached for her sunglasses, allowing her hair to fall around her face. Before she could slip them on, she saw that Trigger was shaking his head. Did that mean he was turning her down? In all honesty, she hadn't once considered that anyone on the list that Crest had given her would pass up a chance to get back into the game. All the info on the men suggested they were hungry for more than what the civilian world could offer. *She* was their chance.

"Well then, I appreciate your time." Catori wasn't a woman to negotiate and she wasn't about to change her position on that topic now. She hadn't lied. Trigger would have made a nice addition to those men she had in mind, but there were other men out there with his skills. She'd have to search a little harder. "Good luck, Trigger."

"Starr, I wasn't implying that I wouldn't take the job." Trigger stood, waving his hand toward the door. She turned to see Diesel sitting a foot away, his head cocked to the side and watching their exchange. "You mentioned you stopped in town. I don't know if you heard, but the owner of this place passed away last week. Mac was like an uncle to me growing up, and when I came back to recuperate, work around the garage gave me something to do. Mac left me the place, along with Diesel."

Catori smothered a curse and slipped on her sunglasses. A dog? It wasn't like Diesel had military training. She turned back around, catching Trigger doing some type of hand motion. He shrugged and smiled, trying to win her over with that Southern charm. It wasn't going to work. Didn't he know that she'd dealt with hundreds of men like him?

"Well, I guess you have your work cut out for you during the next month with selling this place and finding a home for Diesel," Catori stated, making herself clear. "If you accept the position, I'll expect you to report the first of August at the address listed in the email. You'll meet your lead operator and the rest of the team on that date."

"That gives me two months to train Diesel," Trigger said, pushing his luck, and from the look in his brown eyes he knew it. Begrudgingly she respected a man who knew what he wanted and went after it. That still didn't mean he would get his way. "Starr, he's only two years old. I can get it done and he'll be an asset."

"Find him a home, Trigger."

Catori left the office and chose to go out the front door. She flipped the deadbolt and exited, ignoring Diesel's brown eyes. Red had once tried to talk her into getting a canine for their team but she'd adamantly refused. It wasn't cost effective and damned if she'd get too close to an animal that loved so unconditionally. Growing up on a reservation had taught her that. Events happened where people couldn't protect nature and watching it become destroyed was devastating.

"I'll make you a bet, Starr," Trigger called out from the doorway. Catori had her hand on the handle when he'd challenged her. The smart thing would have been to get in her convertible and drive away. Then again, her competitive side came to the forefront and she found herself turning to face him. "If in two months I can get Diesel certified, he comes with me."

"And if you can't?" Catori leaned against the hot surface of her car, crossing her arms as if she had all the time in the world. She could play poker with the best of them. "I don't make bets if there's nothing in it for me, Trigger. And seeing as I know for a fact it takes over a year of basic training with continuous guidance thereafter, the odds are on my side."

"If I lose, I'll foot the bill for the first weekend bender by the team."

"Shit, not good enough. They can pay for their own booze," Catori said, pushing herself off of the vehicle and finally getting situated in the driver's side seat. She pressed the control on the console, not needing a key as the vehicle used a push button ignition. She put her car in reverse and pulled out, shifting back into drive but keeping her foot on the brake. Trigger still stood in the doorway, Diesel by his side. The damn dog looked at her like she'd stolen his only bone. "Two months. If you lose, the entire team paints the new warehouse I purchased for our home base. You can explain the reason their weekends in August are spent on a ladder with a paintbrush."

"Challenge accepted." Trigger flashed a smile that shined through the grease on his chin and cheek. His hand rested on Diesel's head. Damn if she didn't like him already—Trigger, that was. "We'll see you in August, boss."

Catori shook her head, refusing to let the man see her smile. After she hired her lead operator, she'd lean back and watch them be put through their paces. It would be nice to witness the men comprehend that she was the leader Red had always relied on her to be. Thinking it and knowing it were two separate things. She put her foot on the gas pedal and sped down the deserted road toward her next encounter.

Chapter Six

I T HAD TAKEN Catori most of the morning to track down Neal "Doc" Bauer. She'd spent the evening going over the notes and making a list of additional contacts that Red Starr HRT would need in specific embassies. Most of her previous official state department contacts had rotated back to the CONUS—two years was an eternity to be out of the game. The majority of assignments that the federal government wouldn't take were overseas, so it was essential to have reliable associates in key locations. That was also the reason for the *Promised Land*—the ability to park a mobile operating base outside the territorial waters of a hostile country negated the need to transport her team via commercial airlines or slip past corrupt border guards.

The redesigned APD allowed for the midline storage/launch of four eleven meter Naval Special Warfare (NSW) Rigid Hull Inflatable Boats, deployed via an improved articulated boom system that Red had designed himself. In addition to the RHIBs, the refit included the addition of an aft hangar bay facility and a one hundred foot long helo pad for their MH-60S Knighthawk Medium Lift Helicopter. The hangar bay retracted to a twenty-five foot maintenance bay during normal flight operations and expanded to cover an additional twenty-five feet of the flight deck when the Knighthawk was folded and stowed for heavy weather. There were those occasional domestic jobs that didn't require such massive logistical support, but those usually consisted of cults who brainwashed vulnerable people or cases of a similar nature. Either home or abroad, a good communications specialist was vital. Add on the fact that the man she was here in Missouri to see had extensive field medical training and it was a twofer.

"Can I help you, miss?" an elderly gentleman asked. He was wearing a fishing hat with colorful lures hanging on all sides while he maneuvered uphill on the last bit of a dirt path that Catori was certain led away from where the fishing would be. "You seem a little lost."

It appeared to be the question of the week. Catori smiled her appreciation at his offer to help but shook her head. She was wearing jeans. Granted, the shirt she had on wasn't exactly what one would dress out to wet a line. It was a white button-down blouse tapered at the sides. She owned quite a few since they fit so well underneath her jackets. The elderly man didn't blink twice at the weapon on her hip, most likely thinking she was law enforcement.

"I'm just waiting on someone." Catori pushed up her sunglasses and slid them into her hair, mostly to keep the long strands from blowing into her face. A storm front was moving in, and if the dark clouds to the west were any indication it was going to be a big one. "Thank you, though."

Before the older man could ask whom she was meeting, because that was undoubtedly the question on his mind, the sound of a boat's motor could be heard chopping through the water. The man of the hour had just arrived as he expertly steered the rickety fishing boat alongside the only wooden dock within the vicinity. Catori wasn't so sure it should be called a dock though. It resembled more of a ramshackle collection of rotting planks.

Catori and the fisherman watched as Doc used the thick rope to tie off his boat and then shut off the engine. He glanced their way and his piercing green eyes could be seen from where she was leaning against her car. His lean muscular form reminded her of a tiger and his eyes only added to that illusion. His dark blond hair was a mess, but she was relatively sure that was on purpose. It wasn't long, but the thickness gave it a tousled look. He grabbed his gear and stepped onto the unstable anchorage. She was amazed to see that it held his weight.

"Whatever you're here for, trust me, he ain't buyin'." The elderly man gave her a compassionate smile and that's when Catori realized that he thought she was some jilted lover. "He's too hung up on that Charlotte. Shame she left him the way she did."

Catori lifted her eyebrow in question but the fisherman didn't continue. She wasn't the type of person to invade another's privacy. Her pointed look was in the fact that this man was freely giving information to a stranger. He was old enough to know better, but it wasn't her place to chastise him. He'd lived a lot longer than her and he wasn't about to change now.

"Fred, everything all right?" Doc had worked his way up the dirt path to the open area where Catori, and who she now knew was Fred, waited. Doc eyed her red convertible, but not only ignored it afterward but her as well. "Storm is rolling in. You need a lift to Myrna's?"

"No, no," Fred replied, shaking his head. He reached into his back pocket for a rag and wiped the sweat off of his brow. His gnarled fingers had trouble keeping hold of the fabric and Catori had to wonder how he baited a hook. She winced at what she knew must be bad arthritis and didn't envy the daily pain he must live with. "I was just keeping the young lady company."

Young lady? Catori bit her lip to keep from replying that she was fifteen years Doc's senior, but she knew it wouldn't change Fred's perception on age. He had to be entering into his eighties, so to him she was young. Mentally she was anything but. She was still leaning against her car, but she wanted this introduction over so that she could have her say and move on to the next recruit. Holding out her hand, Catori waited for Doc to take it.

"Whatever it is, the answer is no."

"Ha, told ya," Fred said, pulling his lips in, scrunching his face and shaking his head in commiseration.

"Fred, it was a pleasure to meet you." Catori couldn't take any more of the commentary. She let her arm fall back to her side. She needed Doc's full attention, and from the sound of the thunder the storm was almost upon them. "Doc, my name is Catori Starr and I have a proposition for you."

"I already told you the answer's no."

Fred seemed to take the hint, and with a touch to the brim of his hat he slowly meandered on through the lot to his destination. Doc studied her for a moment before turning on his heel, fishing gear in one hand and a pole in the other. Catori did love a challenge. She leaned back against the car and waited until he was about thirty yards out.

"Two thousand and ten. Afghanistan." The year and country brought Doc to a standstill, although he didn't turn around. Catori finally had his attention. He slowly faced her, his green eyes staring at her intently. "Your team lost communication with higher headquarters and was basically on their own to face some serious opposition. You knew friendly fire was about to come from the other side and you managed to get the comms system up and running using only a field expedient NVIS antenna and a reflector you fabricated from the shit laying around your position. You thought outside the box and saved countless lives—which had nothing to do with your medical training, I might add. I need someone with your talent on my team."

"It looks like you're out of luck then. I'm no longer in the service." Doc glanced up at the clouds rolling in. He looked pointedly back at her car. "I'd get the roof up if I were you."

"Red Starr HRT is looking for a comms tech with your skill-set. Your additional medical training is a bonus—one I'm willing to pay extra for." Catori maintained eye contact and baited her trap with his dream. "Your wish of sailing on the ocean with a forty-six foot Perini Navi during retirement could be less than ten years away if you come work for me—although why you would want to retire at such a young age is beyond me."

Catori had sparked his interest now and it was up to her to close the deal before the skies opened up within the next five minutes. The wind had picked up and the trees were swaying in protest. The boat could be heard knocking against the wooden dock and the water had become increasingly choppy.

"Hop in. I'll fill you in on the rest and then drop you off at your house."

Catori knew she'd won when Doc walked her way and around to the passenger side of her convertible. His stride, so like his eyes, was very similar to a tiger as he hunted his prey. She could understand his need to find peace on the water, but he was too young to do it now. He still had many years ahead of him where he could be helping others and she aimed to be the one to utilize him.

"I've heard of Red Starr HRT," Doc said, taking his fishing pole apart into three segments and setting his gear at his feet. She was already situated in the driver's side, pressing the ignition button. By the time Doc was seated, the soft top was closing them in and not a moment too soon. Rain dropped on her windshield. "Why me? There are hundreds of comm specialists out there that could do the job you need filled."

"I want you." Catori pulled the seat belt across the front of her and then shifted the car into gear. She turned the wheels in the direction of town and got them on their way. "Take time to think about it. The offer and contract are sitting in your email for you to review. If you agree to my terms, you'll report the first of August to the address listed."

"Just like that?" Doc placed an elbow against the window while his fingers rubbed his five o'clock shadow. Being a civilian had its perks, but not enough. Catori could see the unreleased energy within just waiting for a chance to break free. "You come out of nowhere, offer me a job, and what?"

"You take it?" Catori countered, maneuvering the small town roads as if she'd been born here. Studying the layout of the town hadn't been that hard. "I'll be honest with you, Doc. Red Starr HRT took a two year break, but now I'm reviving it. Gavin Crest recommended you highly, and seeing as he's one of the few men I trust, here I am."

"Crest?" For the first time since Doc set eyes on her, his shoulders relaxed. Catori had to wonder if there wasn't something she or Crest missed in Doc's background. His body language seemed a little too tense for having just fished an entire morning with nothing else planned for the rest of the day. It almost seemed as if he were expecting trouble. "I've known Crest for quite a few years. He was my Staff NCOIC over in Iraq."

"Forty-eight hours," Catori said, giving a time limit. She already knew he'd say yes, but she wasn't one to like loose threads. The faster her team was formed the quicker it would get her back to San Diego and the chaotic mess her new headquarters had become. Word had already leaked out that Red Starr

HRT was getting ready to take missions and potential assignments were developing. She refused to let her team go on a live operation until she saw how they worked together as a unit. Catori swung the tires of her vehicle until they were side by side with the curb in front of a well-maintained two-story suburban house and shifted into park. "Is there anything you want to tell me that might interfere with the position I'm offering you?"

Doc didn't say anything as he reached down to his feet and grabbed a hold of his fishing gear. It was a damn good thing he kept the tackle box clean. If it had reeked of fish, she'd have made him leave it in his boat. Once he had everything gathered he placed his hand on the handle but didn't move to exit. She waited patiently, her fingers on the stick shift.

"Nothing I can't clean up before the first of August."

Those words didn't necessarily instill the reassurance Catori wanted, but Doc was free to have a personal life. Whatever his situation, it most likely had to do with the woman named Charlotte that Fred had mentioned.

"See to it that it is. I need you focused."

Doc didn't bother to utter another word as he got out of her car. The rain was coming down hard but it didn't seem to bother him as he leisurely took his time to walk up the slightly crooked sidewalk. Catori did notice that he looked around, taking in his surroundings before unlocking his front door. She had a feeling that locking one's home was an unusual occurrence around these parts, but considering what Doc had done for a living, it didn't come as a surprise that he liked the extra security. Having faith in his ability to iron out his personal life before arriving in San Diego, she pulled away from the curb.

Two down, three to go.

Chapter Seven

THE NEON LIT jukebox in the dilapidated bar played a country western tune that was more rock 'n roll in Catori's opinion. It was loud, but not so deafening that the rowdy customers couldn't hear their shouted conversations. It was only eighteen hundred on a weekday, three days after her visit with Doc, but that didn't stop those whom she assumed were regulars from coming in for their daily bellyful. It was a small dive located in a tiny town situated in northern Nebraska.

Catori noticed that the loud banter had become more or less diminished as the locals noticed a stranger amongst them. She quickly memorized the layout of the place, noticing the bar to her right, a dartboard directly toward the back, one pool table off to the left, and around eight tables with four or five chairs each located in the middle. There were two small booths located in the far left corner that would be perfect to have a private conversation. The only potential trouble she could foresee were the two men playing a game of pool. It seemed to her that they might have just reached their limit.

Recognizing her next target, Catori walked directly to the bar and met the gaze of the man she needed to speak with. Daegan Murphy was part Irish and his startling blue eyes were evident of his strong heritage. He kept his head closely shaved to his scalp, but his black hair was unmistakable. The two young girls who couldn't take their eyes off of his six-foot tall muscular frame obviously found him attractive. Catori just wanted him for his ability to button a man's pocket at a thousand yards.

"Daegan, I was hoping you had a moment to speak with me."

"For you, darlin', I have all night." Daegan flipped the hand towel over his shoulder and then folded his arms before leaning on the bar top. "What can I help you with?"

Catori couldn't prevent a smile at his charisma. She had to admit that she was having fun setting up her team. It kept her busy and she found herself feeling closer to Red in doing something that he loved. Seeing the frowns on the faces of the two women who looked as if she had just pissed in their rocks glasses, Catori cut to the chase.

"It's what I can do for you." Catori motioned with her head toward the back booths. "Mind if we talk in private?"

Daegan's smile didn't falter, but she could see that she had his wheels spinning. He tapped the surface of the bar and nodded, giving his consent. Holding up two fingers and gesturing to someone, Catori saw a man at one of the tables stand and head their way. This must be Daegan's brother, Callum. They were similar in their dark good looks, although Callum appeared to have a thinner frame. She also noticed a wedding band on his left hand, making him out of contention with the women.

"This pretty lady would like a word with me, Callum. Mind taking over?"

Callum was more reserved and took the time to look her over, in the direct opposite manner that Daegan had. His brother didn't like strangers in his town and was making it known. When he finally brought his gaze up to meet hers she didn't back down. His lips thinned in annoyance, but he acquiesced and stepped around her to lift a portion of the bar. Callum entered while Daegan exited, but not before Daegan tossed the towel his brother's way.

"After you," Daegan murmured, gesturing with one hand while placing his other on her back. His familiar way was about to be brought to a halt and she wouldn't in any way feel bad about it. In a way it was comical. "What's your name, sweetheart?"

"Catori Starr, of Red Starr HRT."

In under a second Catori felt his hand drop from her waist like his fingers had just been singed. She smiled and kept walking, making her way to one of the empty booths. Picking one, she made sure she was facing the door. Knowing that he would have done the same and seeing the frown mar his face gave her some satisfaction. He slid into his side, giving her one hundred percent of his attention. That was good.

"Red Starr? I thought that agency went defunct a couple years back. What do you want with me?"

"Your services." Catori leaned back against the dark wooden seat and studied Daegan's reaction. "I'm putting together another team. I need a long range shooter with your marksmanship skill."

Daegan sat back as well, mulling over her words. Catori knew damn well that he had an IQ well above average, seeing as he could do the advanced math required for a long distance shot in his head without blinking. He used his charm to cover up exactly how intelligent he was and seemed to enjoy playing with people. She wasn't the woman he wanted to try that on and it was apparent he'd figured that out rather quickly. The smile vanished and he reached over to grab a toothpick from where the holder sat alongside the salt and pepper shakers. Instead of chewing it, he rolled it in his fingers. He was tactile and it showed.

"Why me?"

"Why not you?" Catori countered and then patiently waited for his answer.

"Let's be blunt," Daegan said, pinning her with his blue eyes. "You've obviously read my file. I'm not known to follow orders I don't like. I was transferred out of my unit and into a range PMI billet because I had a difference of opinion with my Ops O. When I detached he shit-canned my career. I was given an adverse fitness report so that I couldn't reenlist. I'm not the sort that Red Starr HRT would be looking for."

"Really?" Catori asked, catching a glimpse of the anger that anyone would have in his position. Daegan had been reassigned from his unit to serve out his time as a primary marksmanship instructor at the base range. He'd only been a civilian for less than a year, but she figured to him it had felt like a lifetime. "And you would know that how?"

"Look, I'm not a machine that someone can program. I use my head. I think, Ms. Starr. I don't regret making that shot against my commander's orders. I took out the target with no other casualties. That was my job and I did it." Daegan tossed the toothpick back onto the table and readied himself to leave. "I appreciate that you would consider me for your team, but you've obviously made a mistake."

"I don't make mistakes, Daegan. I don't believe in mistakes. With that said, I might miscalculate from time to time. We learn something new every day, just as you're about to." Catori picked up the toothpick and held it out for Daegan to take, not continuing until he did so. "First, call me Starr. Second, I want a team of operators who *do* think. Using your head is the only way to ensure that you'll get out of these missions alive. Nothing ever goes as planned, and if one of my men hesitates for a second, when that eventually happens all of your lives are forfeit. I admire your smarts and your gut instinct. Last time. Interested?"

Daegan didn't react at first as he digested what she was offering. When a smile broke out over his face and his blue eyes sparkled, she knew he was hooked. There was an edge about him that suggested he was an adrenaline junkie. As much as he loved his family, as his dossier indicated he wouldn't be satisfied for long working behind a bar.

"Where and when?"

This was the type of negotiation Catori liked. In and out, fast and easy. She quickly recited the same spiel as she had with the other two men, following it up by stating a letter of intent was waiting for him in his email. She also gave her forty-eight hour time limit on her proposition and that should he accept, the day and time he should report to their home base.

"You don't need to wait two days, Starr." Daegan slid out of the booth and held out his hand, for which Catori returned the gesture. "My answer is yes. I'll meet you in San Diego on the first of August."

"Welcome to the team, Daegan." Catori walked toward the bar, seeing that Callum hadn't warmed up during her visit. After hearing what Daegan was going to say, she doubted that she would be Callum's favorite person. That was between the brothers. It was time that she got on the road, and glancing at her watch she was pleased to see she was thirty minutes ahead of schedule. "If you need me beforehand you'll find my number in that email."

"I have no doubt you have mine."

Catori left Daegan at the bar to sort out his family affairs and exited through the door of the bar. Humidity hit her in the face as she continued to walk to her car. She hadn't bothered to roll up the top, seeing as there wasn't rain in the forecast. She wasn't a foot away when she caught sight of something moving in her peripheral vision.

"You're not from around this area." A man in a black ripped T-shirt and a pair of cargo shorts was leaning back against his truck with a cigarette hanging out of his mouth. She wasn't sure if it was to look cool or if it was simply a bad habit. He was one of the good old boys who had been playing pool, and from the empty bottles she'd seen along the rail, he'd started his night early. From his license plate she could say for certain that his name was Lloyd. Catori knew being ahead of schedule was just a fluke. "Want me to show you around?"

"No, thank you." Catori casually looked around, seeing if this guy's friend had decided to join them. It appeared that it was only she and the drunk, so that should make what she had to do relatively easier. She estimated more time to exit civilly. "You have a good evening."

Catori took a step toward her car the same moment that Lloyd moved away from his truck and placed himself between the two vehicles. She gave a half smile at his attempt to intimidate her and then immediately threw a punch to his throat while using the other hand to grab his balls. While he struggled to breathe, she grabbed his shoulder, and using both arms for leverage pulled him close so he heard every word she said.

"You don't want to fuck with me, Lloyd." Catori tightened her grip on his less than average manhood, causing his face to become a darker shade of red and his eyes to widen. "When I let go of you, you're going to move out of my way and allow me passage to my car. If you don't, I'll have to pull out my weapon and your balls really don't want that. Do I make myself clear?"

Lloyd tried to nod, and although the action was more stuttered Catori figured it was a good enough answer. She slowly released him, waiting for any indication that he would be dumber than she assumed he was and actually try something more. He stumbled back a few steps and then turned, quickly making his way around the front of his truck.

Catori pulled on the handle and then slid into the driver's seat. Looking into her rearview mirror, she saw that Daegan was just inside the doorway of the bar, a look of amusement on his face. Although he was closing in on thirty years old, there was something youthful in his appearance that made her feel older than her years. She might actually hole up in a hotel at the first exit she found. Tomorrow would come soon enough.

Chapter Eight

"*O*PEN THOSE BEAUTIFUL *brown eyes of yours, Cat.*"
    Catori struggled to fulfill the request, knowing if she did the likelihood of Red being above her was nonexistent. He wasn't here and never would be again, but she felt his lips against hers now. Lifting her lashes, his gray eyes stared into hers as if the last two years never existed.

    "You aren't real," Catori whispered.

    "As long as you don't let me go I'll always be here. You just need to hold on."

    Not wanting to waste a single second of their time together, real or not, Catori wrapped her arms around Red's neck and brought his lips once more against hers. Kissing him was like breathing…so natural and so graceful it brought tears to her eyes. His soft, warm lower lip always covered hers and sent shivers of anticipation running through her body. As if reading her mind, he trailed his breath down her neck and over her breast, claiming an erect nipple. She tried to arch but suddenly found herself unable to move. She was at his mercy, just the way she liked it.

    "Red, I need to touch you."

    "You aren't taking care of yourself, Cat." The disappointment in Red's voice was palpable and it was like a sharp ache went through her chest. How did he expect her to be? His tongue felt like a blazing torch as it circled her nipple and he finally drew it into his mouth, suckling on the hardened

pebble. Her hands were resting by her head, unable to tangle her fingers into his unruly hair. It was so unfair, especially if she truly awakened to find she'd dreamt this. "I need you healthy. I need you to stay on this newfound path to find…"

Red's voice trailed off as his lips continued exploring. Her body was responding and although she wanted to think his words through, knowing something was wrong with this scenario, she followed his lead into sheer pleasure. His hand gathered up her ample flesh, making it easier to play with her breast. He teased and nibbled on the sensitive tissue until she was crying out his name.

As if the sound of her voice triggered this fantasy to deviate courses, Catori found herself on top of Red, looking down into his striking face. Gray eyes that resembled a storm rolling in from the west were just as restless as the menacing clouds that gathered above. Before she could question this apparition, she felt her body accepting him. Her knees were on either side of him and his cock was stretching her sheath, creating that burn that she'd come to relish.

"Take me like you always do, Cat." Red's fingers felt like they were digging into her side, although she also felt them on her breasts. The sensations were almost too much to calculate, so she concentrated on what she could do. "Sink your nails into my chest."

Catori did as he asked and used his chest for leverage. Red's contoured muscles gave her fingers something to hold on to as she continued to sink over his cock, over and over until finally she'd accepted all of him. Gyrating to truly feel his presence was the only way she could savor these precious moments. She needed to feel the sting from his width and cried out when she started to feel the quivers in her pussy, indicating her need to come.

"You know your orgasm is stronger if I'm taking you from behind," Red whispered in her ear. She abruptly found herself on her hands and knees. Catori loved this position because his cock went farther into her core, producing a stronger and amazingly intense release. She dug her nails into the sheets as he took control by sliding his fingers into her hair and drawing

her head back. "Do you remember how kinky we could be, Cat?"

Various images of their past rushed through her while Red pounded into her from behind. Without slowing his thrust or releasing his hold on her hair, she felt something on her clit. This should have awakened her, yet her body was too far gone wrapped up in Red's memory. Long strokes over her engorged flesh drew out an animalistic moan from deep within her. No one else could make her feel like this.

Catori was suddenly lowered to the bed, with her ass still in the air and her pussy taking Red's cock like he hadn't been gone for two years. She rested her cheek against the cool sheets, knowing that Red had total control over this fantasy. There were times they wrestled for power, and as fun as that had been, there was something euphoric when Red actually won.

Her cream was now dripping down her inner thigh and her clit was receiving so much pleasure that it bordered on pain. This had to be real. The sensations were overwhelming and were becoming almost magical. Her body felt like it was floating as Red continued to make love to her. There wasn't a place on her warm flesh that hadn't been touched in some way.

"Come for me."

Catori opened her mouth to draw in air when her release hit, but it was useless. She gathered up more of the rumpled sheets in her fists as her body exploded. Red's cock felt like it expanded inside of her as waves of contractions rippled around his shaft. Like always, he never let up on her clit either as he knew that only prolonged her orgasm.

"You need to come for me…"

"I did!" Catori cried out, sitting straight up in bed and looking around wildly. Perspiration dripped down the side of her cheek and she swiped away her damp hair, catching her breath and trying to make sense of what had just occurred. The hotel room was empty, with only the air conditioning making noise if she discounted her hard respiration. "Shit."

It had felt so real. Catori didn't need to look down at her

nipples to know they were hard and that her panties were damp. With trembling hands, she pulled the white tank top she'd been sleeping in over her head, trying to cool down. Had she truly come from just a dream? They were becoming so real lately that if she hadn't embarked on this new journey to reopen Red Starr's doors she would have thought she was losing her mind. Work had given her something to do and she had thought that it would quell these dreams. It wasn't like she didn't want to feel Red and keep this part of him, but she *knew* that it wasn't real and that scared her most of all. She could handle fear, but she couldn't take feeling downright frightened of…some type of premonition. That's what it had felt like, but she couldn't put her finger on why.

Glancing at the clock, Catori debated on whether she should shower and start her day early. Four o'clock in the morning was a little excessive, but there were people who would be awake by now who would be able to assist her in checking off some of the items on her to-do list. She ignored the exhaustion that was settling in her bones. She knew that she was replacing one bad habit with another, but she didn't care. Work was becoming her salvation and once things were in full swing, she would settle into a normal routine. She would.

Chapter Nine

THREE DAYS LATER, Catori found herself in the state of Washington. Her original destination had been to drive to Wyoming and visit Aaron "Stick" Scott at his home, but he didn't make it easy on her. Wasting this much time didn't make her happy and she damn well hoped that this man was worth every minute she'd lost. She pulled alongside a couple of trucks before shutting off her engine and exiting her convertible.

The temperature wasn't as warm here as it was in the Midwest, so she was thankful that she'd brought more than a couple of blazers on this trip. This red one was a little longer than the others and while it had a cloth type belt the edge of her jacket fit over her weapon a little easier. It wasn't even sunrise yet, but from what she'd gathered, if she didn't catch Stick this morning she wouldn't have a chance to speak with him for the next six months.

The diner's lights lit up the wharf as bells from the ships tinkered and their engines hummed. Catori walked toward the lively eatery, scouting for Aaron Scott through the windows. She caught sight of him at the counter, finishing up what he thought was going to be his last meal on land for the next twenty-four weeks. He didn't realize it yet, but his luck was about to change.

"Excuse me," a man mumbled after he'd opened the door and signaled his exit with the chime above their heads.

Catori used it to her advantage and smiled her appreciation for his politeness in holding the door open for her. She closed the distance to the counter and took the empty seat next to Stick. He didn't look up from his coffee cup, which appeared to have only one more drink left. Sure enough, he swallowed the contents and then reached behind for his wallet.

"We can technically call this a business meeting," Catori said, placing her hand on the written ticket laying by his plate and sliding it her way. Finally she'd garnered his attention. Unlike Doc's darker blond hair, Stick's was lighter and he still maintained his military cut. He'd let it grow out slightly on top, making her immediately think of the surfer model photographers used for ads at the beach. His blue eyes met hers and it was obvious he wasn't anywhere near the free spirit of a surfer. "Mind if we take this conversation somewhere private?"

"I don't think so," Stick replied, resuming taking out his wallet and pulling out some cash. He threw three five-dollar bills onto the counter and then stood, returning his billfold back from where he got it. He did have the courtesy to nod his appreciation for her gesture before turning to go. "Have a nice day, ma'am."

"I find it interesting that a man with your many talents would waste them out on an oil rig in the middle of the ocean. I'd think it would get boring after a while. Same smells, same view." Catori saw a booth opening up toward the back and stood with every intention of claiming it. She took a couple steps, making no effort to ensure that he would follow. "As for being incommunicado for that length of time, that's got to be hard on you and your family, Stick."

Catori didn't look back as she made her way to the booth,

taking the seat facing the door. It was comical to watch the men's faces as they realized she'd done it on purpose. She knew better than to have her back toward an open room without being able to see what was coming. Stick was still standing by his stool, contemplating his options. She'd piqued his interest enough that he finally conceded and joined her at the table.

"Who are you?"

"Catori Starr, Red Starr HRT." She held her arm over the table and shook his hand, noticing that his grip was firm. He didn't lessen the tension just because she was a woman. She liked that. "I've got to tell you, I didn't expect to be chasing your ass over two states, so you better be as good as Crest tells me."

"Crest?" Stick relaxed slightly at the name. Now she definitely had his full attention. "How is that old son of a bitch? I haven't seen him in quite a few years."

"I know," Catori replied, signaling with two fingers to the waitress that she'd like two cups of coffee. "He's his usual cryptic self. Makes a person want to knock his block off, but he'd probably put me on my ass. I'm good, but not so sure I'm *that* good. Of course, the element of surprise might be in my favor."

"Hostage Rescue Team?" Stick had been paying attention. Another plus. "Why would you be interested in me?"

"Why did you leave the Corps?" Catori pulled back, allowing the waitress to set a mug in front of both of them. Conveying the two of them were good for a while, the waitress left them alone. "You only had eight years left until retirement."

"If you spoke with Crest, you know that I was a foot stomper. EOD—explosives ordinance disposal." Stick looked out the window, where the sun didn't show a hint of rising. It reminded Catori of all those early mornings in the Corps. "I'd had enough."

"Just like that?" Catori sipped her coffee, a few degrees hotter than the normal pot of coffee. She was surprised it wasn't bubbling. "You up and quit?"

"Quit?" Stick's blue eyes darkened at her implication and he leaned forward, placing his elbows on the table. "I served my country for twelve years disposing of landmines, cluster bomb sub munitions, unexploded ordinances of every kind and make you can imagine—from improvised explosive devices in Iraq to our own AT4 rounds that skittered across the ground and laid there until someone walked by. All it took was for someone's shadow to make the temperature vary on those fuckers and have them explode. I didn't quit, Ms. Starr. I was smart enough to know my name was written on one of those and I knew it was only a matter of time until I met my maker."

"You think you have a few more to defuse before you find your name? I know it's a gamble, but look on the bright side. If you take me up on what I'm about to offer, you'll be using those weapons for their intended purpose instead of disarming them. It'll be a change of scenery and one you might like." Catori could finally take a well-deserved drink of caffeine since the coffee had cooled by less than a quarter of a degree. "By the way, it's just Starr."

"Fine." Stick threw his hands up and then sat back, giving Catori his full attention. "Tell me this offer of yours."

"I'm gathering up a team to reassemble Red Starr HRT from the ground up. It was and will remain a first class operation. I want you on my squad." Catori continued to talk, going into more specifics and knowing that what she was offering was too good for him to pass by. "You would make enough over the next five years to see to it that your sister receives the treatment she needs. I can only imagine how hard it is for your family to give twenty-four hour care. So I see it two ways. One, you can

go back to working the oil rigs and be away for six months at a
time. They pay well. Or two, you can come work for me and
make five times what you do here, have the ability to come
home between missions, and know that I'd pull your ass out
ASAP if something happened to either your sister or parents."

Catori waited for her proposition to sink in, enjoying the rich
flavor of the coffee. Damn if it wasn't one of the best she'd had
in months. She'd have to get some to go, knowing she could
make it to California by nightfall. She needed to make a stop in
the northern part of the state to finish up her business before
heading down to San Diego by tomorrow.

"So what's it going to be, Stick?" Catori would normally
have given her forty-eight hour window, but if she caught up
with Kane Taylor either tonight or tomorrow she wanted to be
able to give him a file of the team he would be leading for the
next five years. Her contracts were iron clad, so unless one of
them ended up dead—which was certainly a possibility—they
would all be working for Red Starr HRT for their foreseeable
future. "Red wire or green wire?"

"Fuck." Stick ran both hands over his face as if this were a
hard decision. Catori wasn't seeing it, but if he'd like to make a
production out of it that was his choice. She wouldn't claim to
understand what it was like to have a sister who'd been paralyzed
from the neck down in a car accident. What she could do was
offer him enough money that his family wouldn't feel the effects
of having to care for someone twenty-four seven. She finished
off her coffee and then signaled once again to the waitress,
although this time she indicated a to-go cup. "It's a good offer,
Starr."

"Any reason you're hesitating?"

"Other than it places me back in the same situation as I was
before? It wasn't necessarily a bomb that had my name written

on it. A bullet would do the job."

"It could," Catori agreed, not able to make Stick the guarantees he obviously wanted. It wasn't like he thought he would get them, but she could understand his uncertainty. That didn't mean she wouldn't get the answer she wanted. "Or you could drown out in the middle of the fucking ocean on some shit box oilrig."

Stick laughed, the weight of the world easing from his shoulders slightly. He took responsibility to heart and his family meant the world to him. She knew from his dossier that he felt the same about his unit and even to this day still kept in contact with some of them. He would be an asset to her team in many, many ways. When he smiled and leaned back, lacing his hands behind his head, she knew she'd won another round.

"Green. Count me in."

Chapter Ten

"KANE TAYLOR."

Catori grimaced when the machines kept roaring, drowning out her voice and everything else with it. The construction crew must have already had their morning break seeing as they were all actually working and doing their jobs. This must be one hell of a ramrod for a foreman. Orange vests and hard hats were the only thing visible as the crew went about rebuilding a bridge. She didn't want to know what they were doing, not caring in the slightest. As long as what was already up didn't fall into the damn water she'd consider the morning a success. It wasn't that she wasn't prone to dangerous situations, but purposefully walking a metal plank to her death wasn't going to be one of them.

"Taylor's over in the trailer. Now get the hell off my site."

At least that's what Catori thought the hard-edged foreman said. She breathed a sigh of relief as she walked back the distance to where the trailer was situated off the side of the road, far away from the bridge and nestled into a patch of grass. The cloud coverage kept the heat at bay, and if anything the air had a slight chill to it. She'd just reached for the handle of the door when it sprang open, revealing the man she was looking for.

"Who are you?" Kane barked, not bothering to pause in his stride as he pushed past.

"Catori Starr." She looked Taylor over as he stepped down from the trailer and turned. According to his basic information his formidable form was six foot three and two hundred thirty pounds of solid muscle. His dark brown hair was still cut with the same military style as the day he'd retired a rank below her as a Gunnery Sergeant. He was older than the others on her team, although not more senior than she was, and he'd also seen more action and knew how to lead a squad into Indian country. He was a born leader of warriors and she was about to give that opportunity back to him. "Mind if we step back into the trailer where we can have a conversation without losing our voices?"

"Talk all you want, but I'm not buying what you're selling." Kane didn't bother stopping to see if she'd catch up with him. Hell, with his attitude he probably thought she'd scurry off due to his rude manner. She could appreciate where he was coming from, but ground rules were about to be set into place. She would get final say when he was under her employment and that was about to become apparent. Kane pulled the cheap Motorola Talkabout from his belt and shouted into the transmitter. "Sully, did you get those blueprints like I asked? The rest of this bridge isn't going to build itself and we can't do shit without those plans."

Catori let Kane walk away, his voice deep and resonating over the volume of the machines. Complaints about Sully could be heard loud and clear as he sought out the man in question. That wasn't her concern and frankly she hadn't had quite enough caffeine to have to deal with this. She leaned against the trailer, knowing the white crisp-starched shirt she pulled out of her suitcase this morning would be black from the dirt that was caked onto the siding. Waiting for one of the construction crew to walk by, she was finally able to stop one of the men and motioned with her hand that she wanted his walkie-talkie.

Catori bided her time and waited for just the right moment—which was when Kane was about to climb into a black Ford 150 truck that looked brand spanking new. She lingered a moment more for him to open the door and set a boot-clad foot onto the runner before she pressed the button on the side of the radio.

"Gunny, I have a team assembled and they are awaiting orders. Your orders." Catori released the button and observed Kane's reaction from afar. He stopped and slowly lowered his foot to the ground. Although she couldn't see them from here, she knew his hazel eyes now bore into her. She pressed the switch one more time. "Unless you'd rather stay here and, you know, build a bridge. I wouldn't want you to miss all this action. *Interrogative.*"

It didn't surprise Catori when Kane walked back her way and his stride struck her like a predator on the prowl. The use of the single word on a tactical radio channel meant she had asked a question and expected a response. She remained where she was until he was standing in front of her, the intensity of his stare trying to gauge what she meant. She maintained his gaze as she held out the radio to the man still standing beside her, who looked like he'd rather be anywhere but here. He looked at Kane before slowly reaching for the walkie-talkie and quickly walked away toward the bridge.

"Seems like you run a tight ship here, although your talents are wasted in my opinion."

"I don't care about random people's opinions," Kane replied, surveying Catori from head to toe. He kept his judgments well hidden. "You've captured my attention though. No one has called me Gunny in a couple of years. I take it this is a government sanctioned job?"

"Does that mean your skills are rusty?" Catori asked, ignoring his question. She gave as good as she got and took her time looking Kane over from top to bottom. He was a very attractive man, although not her type in the slightest. Red's face flashed before her eyes, bringing her back to why she was here. "I'm sure there are other Gunnery Sergeants who served and whom can still step up to the plate."

"Like I said, you've got my attention." Kane reached for the handle of the door, which was to the right of where Catori was standing, and opened the flimsy access. He motioned for her to proceed before him, and once both of them were inside the trailer he shut them inside. Other than the whirl of the AC unit pushing air into the room, it was fairly quiet. It took time for her eyes to adjust and she was surprised to see that the depth of the trailer was actually bigger than it appeared. "Coffee?"

"No, thank you." Catori took a seat at a small wooden table that had seen better days. She knew from his attitude that Kane wasn't the type of man who liked to sit for long moments of time, so she cut to the chase. "In your email you'll find a five year contract for the position of lead operator working for me at Red Starr HRT. We take hostage rescue missions that the Bureau won't touch or can't legally touch. To answer your question, we're not government sanctioned—however, we do have a license to operate in the US and abroad. I don't have to tell you that some of the assignments that we'll take will be risky, whereas others should be a piece of cake. Luck of the draw— you see, Red Starr HRT is a private contractor. Our services don't come cheap. You come highly recommended and from what I've read in regards to your assignments, your skillset is well matched with the team that I've assembled."

"Red Starr HRT." Instead of sitting with her at the table,

Kane leaned back against a counter that appeared as if it would crack from the weight of his body. He crossed his arms and she wasn't surprised to see the size of his biceps. He wasn't the type of man to let his body get out of shape and she had to wonder if he'd always known he would get back into the combat life somehow, someway. "I met your husband Red a while back. I was sorry to hear that he had come up MIA."

"You don't have to fill his shoes," Catori said in reassurance, although she knew Kane hadn't given his condolences for that purpose. She didn't really care. She wanted a team. He was that last spot, and if he didn't want to take it that was fine by her. "Your job will be to lead and train a freshly assembled tactical team. Are you interested?"

"Do I get a say in the members of this team?"

"Within reason—however, I make the final call on every team member." Catori could just make out the tightening of Kane's jaw, indicating his displeasure at not having the definitive decision on the men that he would be responsible for. "Make no mistake, Kane, I make the final call as to who is on our crew as well as all of the assignments. When you're in the field, the tactical decisions are solely yours. You trust me to give you the tools and training you need and I'll trust for you to get the job done with the least amount of casualties to our team."

Silence descended over the small trailer, and while Catori allowed Kane time to digest the information that she'd laid out in front of him she glanced at her watch. She had set up a meeting with a heavy weapons supplier later this evening and as of right now she was doing okay on time. Before Kane made a decision, she wanted to go over one more thing that she was well aware wouldn't be a pleasant topic. She knew this from personal experience.

"Your sister was killed during a deployment over in Nigeria."

At this point, Catori was sure that Kane's jaw would crack under the pressure he was employing on it. This was something she had to cover, so she continued. "I understand that Sidney had been chosen for an op and that you were against it. You've ruffled some feathers lately in wanting answers that no one seems willing to give."

"This isn't a topic that I'm going to discuss with you." Kane kept his reply short, as if he thought that would end this conversation. "Much like Red is off limits around you, my sister has the same status."

"Duly noted." Catori felt each and every one of his words as if she'd just taken a bullet to her chest. It didn't change the circumstance of needing to have this discussion. "*After* you give me the reassurance I need, we don't need to bring this up again."

"And what reassurance would that be?" Kane inquired, his voice void of any emotion.

"You won't use Red Starr's operational access to obtain the answers you seek." Catori stood and slipped her hands into the back pockets of her jeans, conveying a relaxed appearance when she felt anything but. She knew exactly how Kane suffered and there was nothing on the face of this earth that could give him the closure he needed. "We have military and government contacts that have extremely high and very special clearances, even as contractors. We'll utilize them for our missions, such as our secure Siprnet server, encryption systems, and feeds from NRO for Tactical Data. These relationships that I've cultivated and hardware I've gained access to aren't to be used for personal reasons. I won't risk the lives of my team because you've burned bridges we need to operate."

"And if I can't guarantee that?"

Catori distinguished from reviewing Kane's dossier that he was a man of honor and spoke only the truth. She respected that and had been prepared for it as well. Men like him were the reason others survived situations that would otherwise have failed. She was always willing to compromise, given that it benefited both parties.

"I give you my word that *I* will look into your sister's death if you give me your word that you won't jeopardize the affiliations that we've worked damn hard for at Red Starr HRT." Catori waited for her words to sink in, and when the brown of his hazel eyes became more golden, she knew they had a deal. That didn't mean she didn't want a verbal promise. "I'll need your word."

"It would be hard for me to turn down that kind of offer, Starr." Kane slowly extended his arm. "Which is why you have yourself a deal."

Catori firmly shook his hand, emotions swirling inside of her that she'd actually just solidified her Alpha team. She wasn't in the mood to sort them out, nor did she want to. There were still things that needed to be done and the effort to get this collection organized into a cohesive fighting unit would keep her and him busy.

"My team...I want to look over their profiles."

"As I stated, their details have been emailed to you. If you have any questions or concerns, please feel free to contact me. My cell phone number is included. You have forty-eight hours to sign and return the letter of intent." Catori headed for the exit and opened the door, allowing in the loud construction noises as well. She stepped down and then turned on her heel to find Kane still leaning up against the counter. "Your team reports on the first of August at exactly zero seven hundred. I suggest you arrive the week before so we're able to go over their training schedule, inventory the team bunkhouse, inspect the hardware that will be available to us, and the software that we'll be using. We have a support system staff of well over fifty personnel and that doesn't include the ship's crew or the flight crew for our new Knighthawk."

"I'll be there."

Catori closed the door, giving Kane the privacy he needed to digest what she had offered him and the agreement that he'd made. She was confident that he wouldn't change his mind, but she also knew that the next time she saw him he'd question her about what she'd discovered regarding his sister. Catori had already put feelers out and the preliminaries coming back weren't good. Something FUBAR had occurred and Sidney Taylor had gotten caught in the crossfire.

Walking to her car, Catori pulled out her phone and skimmed through her contacts. Finding the one person who might be able to help and highlighting their name, she pressed the call button. As the line rang, she pulled on the handle of her convertible and settled into the driver's seat. She continued to stare at the trailer while she waited for her contact to answer.

"Catori Starr," Schultz Jessalyn announced, as if he was surprised to hear from her. "To what do I owe this pleasure?"

"Cut the bullshit, Schultzy," Catori replied with a smile as she saw Kane finally leave the trailer. "We both know you are well aware that I am forming another team. My bet is you have a list of my crew already on your desk and you know the precise reason that I'm calling."

"You never were any fun." Schultz Jessalyn was currently the Special Assistant to the National Security Advisor for the President of the United States. His title was a mouthful and fit his personality to a tee. He was a complex man and one that she would never want to make an enemy of. She'd lucked out though, and Schultz happened to be a damn good friend, which was the only reason she had his personal phone number. "Leave it buried."

Catori didn't take any pleasure in being right and she felt her frustration mount. She understood and could sympathize with Kane in regards to his sister. She leaned her head back against the padding of her seat, hearing the warning that Schultz was giving her but also knowing when something wasn't right.

"I can't afford to be kept in the dark on this one, Schultzy— especially when it involves the family of my new lead operator." Catori watched as Kane walked up to a man carrying a set of blueprints and start up a conversation. She tried to word her inquiry carefully. "If whatever happened has the potential to cause damage to Red Starr HRT, I have a need to know right now…her brother has a right to know if some shit-stain blew his assignment and greased his sister."

"Not everything should be public knowledge, Starr." Schultz wasn't going to budge on this. If it was one thing Catori hated, it was not seeing the hand she was playing with. "This is one that you need to let go of for everyone's sake."

"I can't do that." Catori tried to figure out a way to negotiate for the information, but having taken two years off had depleted her resources. "Taylor deserves some answers, Schultz, even if it's just a thread."

"We both know that one lone strand can lead to a complete shit storm breaking loose." A long pause blanketed the phone and Catori resisted the urge to pull the cell away from her ear to see if the line was still connected. She remained silent, hoping he'd cave but knowing he was protecting his interests. Because of that, his next statement surprised her. "I'll have something for you by the end of the week."

The only reason Schultz would divulge classified and potentially threatening information was if he wanted something in return. An ominous cloud was settling over her mood and her gut reaction said she wasn't going to like the outcome. These men deserved better—Taylor deserved better—and she would see to it that nothing blemished their new beginning.

"Favors are returned in kind," Catori reminded Schultz, wanting to make her position clear. "I expect sufficient information…enough to ease Taylor's mind."

"I'll obtain what I can, but I can't guarantee it will be what he wants to hear."

Catori closed her eyes, wishing that Schultz hadn't added on that last part. If Sidney Taylor had been used as a chess piece by the higher powers involved, Kane wasn't the type let justice escape from his hands. This was setting up to become a clusterfuck of mega proportions and she had a decision to make. Did she get out of the car and rescind her offer? Would it be better for the morale and safety of her team? She immediately rejected that thought, knowing full well that Taylor deserved justice. If she got her hands a little dirty helping him achieve that, so be it.

"I would say thank you for your assistance, but I have a feeling this is going to cost me." Catori watched as Kane headed to his truck. His eyes had caught sight of her red convertible the minute he'd stepped out of the trailer and he made no effort to hide his scrutiny now. She hoped like hell that no one was alive that had a hand in his sister's death. If they were, they'd be begging for mercy soon enough. "Try to keep it unproblematic."

"Ah, Starr, you know I won't promise you that," Schultz stated, disconnecting their call with a laugh.

Catori sat there a while longer, watching Kane's truck make a U-turn and fade away as he traveled down the road. He had the right idea in mind—they both had a lot of things that needed to be accomplished, and sitting here in the middle of a construction zone wasn't going to get the job done. As she'd come to realize, the world kept spinning while one's personal life was experiencing upheaval. The secret was to move with the general population while simultaneously dealing with the grief that reality had dealt. Vengeance didn't bring one peace, but it sure as hell made a Marine feel as if he'd satisfied the mission requirements.

Chapter Eleven

CATORI TOOK HER cup of tea out onto her deck overlooking the Pacific Ocean. This beachfront house had been her and Red's home for when they had been between missions. She couldn't bring herself to sell it and eventually let the lease run out for the apartment they'd rented in the city for some of their quick overnights. The last month had given her pause to consider leasing another one, but she quickly rejected the idea. Instead she made sure the construction crew rebuilding the interior of Red Starr HRT's new headquarters had included some additional living space attached to her office where she could overnight if called upon. This was where she felt Red and this was where she would stay, regardless of the drive.

The large round patio sat high off the ground, with ten steps that led down to the cliff face that overlooked the sand and waves below. The reason she and Red had purchased this property was the feeling of isolation and the natural beauty that surrounded them. The white wooden spirals were set twelve inches apart and easily offered a view of the terrain. There was a small path that led down to the beach, but Catori didn't feel like taking a walk tonight. Instead she opted to sit in one of the chairs that rarely got used nowadays. The temperature had been in the high seventies, but at this time of night there was a cool Santa Ana breeze coming in off of the ocean. She'd known it would be this way and had grabbed her favorite sweater as always.

Catori had just settled herself into one of the Tuscan colored cushioned chaise lounges and taken a sip of her tea when the phone rang. She didn't hurry as she placed her tea on the side table, knowing exactly who it was on the other line and not feeling any urgency to hear the triumph in his voice. Sure enough, Gavin Crest's name appeared on the display.

"Take your gloating somewhere else," Catori replied into her cell. Crest's rich laughter floated out of the speaker and into the air. "Unless you're calling for another reason, I don't want to hear it."

"I don't gloat."

"Bullshit."

"Are you trying to stir up the hornet's nest?"

"Schultzy called you?" Catori sat up a little straighter, trying to connect the dots but coming up blank. "Are you fucking serious?"

"No, he didn't. You called Schultzy?" Crest's exasperation was evident. "Shit, Starr, nothing is worse than owing that man a favor."

"Kane Taylor deserves to know the truth," Catori stated, not apologizing for the steps she'd taken. "His sister was killed on that mission and her superiors aren't being truthful with him. It's in the best interests of my team to have his head clear and unburdened. If Schultzy didn't call you then how did you find out that I was nudging for the facts?"

"I received a call from a full bird colonel who ran that operation, thinking I had something to do with the interest of certain classified information." Crest paused, as if evaluating how much he should share with her. She didn't appreciate his evasiveness in the least. "It was an obvious assumption on his part, considering he was the one I obtained information from regarding Kane Taylor."

"So Kane worked under this colonel when he was in the service?"

"Nice try, but that's not going to work." Crest wasn't irresponsible and Catori had never bore witness to him falling for something as simple as a leading question. It hadn't stopped her from trying. "Starr, I've got a bad feeling about that botched mission. I don't want it coming back and ruining your fresh start if something gets made public that never should have seen the light of day."

"If this was one of your team members, you wouldn't hesitate to do some digging yourself," Catori pointed out, knowing they were alike in that way. Loyalty, honesty, support, and trust were vital among a unit. Her crew would know that going in and, God help them, going out. "Kane needs answers and I have the contacts and wherewithal to give him closure."

"Schultzy? Damn, woman, you didn't go for the handgun— you went directly for the Howitzer."

"Have you ever known me to be subtle? Why settle for a flyswatter when a surface to air missile will do?" Catori settled back into her chair and picked up tea. It had gotten lukewarm but it still tasted good. "Besides, someone's got to keep that man out of trouble."

"He'll be happy as a fucking lark alright whenever he needs your services as payback."

"Nothing I can't handle." Catori felt the years drain away and it was as if she was back in time, waiting for Red to join her out here on the patio. Crest had been a frequent visitor and this camaraderie between them felt familiar and comforting.

"Schultzy likes to keep in contact with us lowly civilians. He gets bored up in the White House. I'm only helping out."

"It's a good way to get your ass burnt with one of his fly-by-night black bag specials."

"Speaking of which, have you gotten any ass lately? Last time you mentioned anyone was when you and Schultzy had that State Department dinner in D.C."

"I still see her from time to time, but only when I'm in D.C. on business. Getting CSA off the ground is keeping me busy." Crest's bachelor status was well known among their circles and Starr looked forward to when some woman had the wherewithal to tame him. "Besides, who wants an old scourge like me? Speaking of personal lives, if things get too heated when Taylor finds out what really happened over in Nigeria, don't hesitate to give me a call."

"Did this colonel tell you something that you'd like to share?" Catori asked, her mind spinning of what could have happened that forced a high-ranking official to cover it up.

"No," Crest replied, "he was vague. It was apparent he wasn't willing to shed light on the situation without considerable pressure. Which leads me to offering you the advice I originally called about—it would be in Red Starr HRT's best interest to let it go. Even an old dim-witted jarhead like me knows when to pull back."

Tea sputtered out of her mouth as another infrequent laugh took hold. She pulled the phone away from her ear and used the back of her hand to wipe the drips running down her chin. She used her other hand to put the cup back on the side table. Once she could inhale without feeling like she was drowning, she eventually put the cell back to her ear.

"Crest, you've never known when to pull back a day in your whole fucking life." Catori shook her head at the absurdity of his statement. "Shit, it's your ass that Red always had to pull out of the fire."

"Yes, he did." Crest's voice had softened and it dawned on Catori that this was the first time she'd brought up her husband in talking about the past in such a casual manner. It made her chest hurt and she was appreciative when Crest ended the call. "If you need me, all you have to do is call. God knows that I still owe you a favor or two. Good night, Starr."

Catori lowered the phone from her ear and slowly placed it next to her now half empty cup of tea. Earlier this evening she'd been satisfied with her initial progress in reviving a company that made this world a better place. She could separate that part of her life. What she didn't like was this transition that seemed to be happening to her personally. She wasn't ready to let go of Red. She wasn't ready to refer to him in the past tense.

Catori closed her eyes and listened as the waves crashed against the sand in the distance. It amazed her that two oceans could sound so different, although she admitted that maybe it had something to do with the memories. This was where she and Red had built their home. This was the stability that they'd needed and in which had been taken away with one FUBAR mission that should have been a cakewalk.

She wasn't averse to the fact that Kane Taylor was facing something similar today that she'd had to deal with two years ago. Catori still felt that she'd missed something in regards to Red and the team's elimination. No matter whom she contacted, no matter how many times she'd questioned the liaison that assisted Red Starr HRT, and no matter how many satellite images she'd spent hours combing over…she never did receive a concise answer as to what had truly transpired to cause the mission to go south. If Kane Taylor didn't need to suffer the same fate, then she would assist him in any way that she could.

What seemed like hours later Catori couldn't keep her eyes open anymore. She'd resorted to her old habit of sitting out here and trying to obtain some of the peace that the ocean seemed to bring every once in a while. She wasn't sure of the time. She only knew that she was tired enough to get a few hours of sleep without having a nightmare that relived the day she'd found out about Red. She welcomed the sleep and managed to move her numb ass off of the lounge and into the house.

The morning would be here soon enough and she was certain that Kane Taylor would be at the warehouse facility at zero six hundred. Most of the construction was done with the new office spaces, armory, security fences, pier upgrades, an extremely large maintenance bay, attached hangar, training areas, team bunkhouse, communications electronics suite, briefing room, and a state of the art operations control facility. If she worked enough hours tomorrow then maybe, just maybe, she wouldn't have to sit out here staring into the darkness until exhaustion overtook her.

"CAT," RED'S DEEP voice called out, the raspy coarseness of it sending shivers over her skin. Was he really here with her? Catori's eyes fluttered open and sure enough, he was situated above her with his sexy crooked smile and blue eyes. His blond hair was tousled and the fiery highlights could be seen even in the golden hued lighting coming from her bedside table. Something told her this wasn't real, yet she couldn't stop herself from reaching out with her hand and gently placing her palm directly on his whiskered cheek. Would he disappear? "Cat, I'm still here."

A sob rose up inside of Catori's chest because she knew that he wasn't. Red was gone but that didn't mean she wouldn't take these special moments when he chose to appear to her. He lowered his head and brushed his lips against hers, so softly and so tenderly that she could hardly feel it. There was a reason for that, but she pushed that thought out of her mind. She would be greedy just this once.

Using her tongue, she traced his lips...knowing them from memory. The fullness of his mouth was engrained on every part of her skin. He used to explore to his heart's content, always making her beg for more. Catori moved her head to the side, wanting to feel the heat from his mouth on her neck. It was there, she just knew it. Discarding all thought, she abandoned herself to his memory, his touch, his being.

Red caressed the side of her breast and his calloused fingers brought with them a trail of fire. Yes, she could sense everything he was doing. Catori opened her eyes to see him dip his head and felt her nipple enveloped in the moist heat of his mouth. Nothing had ever felt so pleasurable and she arched her back, trying to receive more. He loved nibbling on her, yet he wasn't doing that. She strained for that slight erotic pain that he liked to give.

"More, Red. I need more."

"I'll give you whatever you want, Cat." Red smiled lovingly and he once again dipped his head, her abdomen recognizing the blazing trail of his tongue as he went lower. It felt like he was becoming more real with each stroke, caress, and kiss. This couldn't end. She felt alive and loved. She wanted to stay in this realm of existence forever. "That's right. Feel me."

Red separated her legs and situated himself in between her thighs. His masculine form was suddenly unclothed, revealing his contoured chest. Catori didn't care how it happened or why. She ran her hands down his biceps, loving how solid his muscles were underneath her touch. His sun-kissed skin seemed to glow and she traced the hard lines of his flat stomach to where a sensual V led into the treasure that she sought.

"Are you ready for me, Cat?"

"Red, I need you now more than ever." Catori wrapped her legs around his waist, trying to draw him near. He wouldn't move but instead stared down at her with a caring smile. She wanted to take control and memories flashed through her mind with the battle of wills they used to have, making *them laugh like children. There was no laughter now…just intense need. She had to take the lead. "Let me ride you. Let me take control."*

"Even using your claws wouldn't convince me to let you do that, Cat. Do you remember? Do you recall how we used to wrestle on this bed until the sheets were tangled?" Red gradually lowered himself until Catori felt his cock slowly enter her. He stretched her wide and the slight burn almost caused her to have an orgasm right then and there. "Are your claws out? You know I like it when you scratch my back."

Pleasure filled every pore of Catori's body as Red gently thrust in and out of her. He leaned his head down once more and she swore his teeth bit into her nipple like he used to do. A cry of pleasure escaped her lips, and when she tried to hold him in place his gentle laughter filled the air. She wanted to be on top, to take control.

"Claws, Cat. I want to feel your claws."

Catori felt helpless, for she tried to do what Red said but her fingers couldn't get a firm hold on him. She looked up and saw the love in his eyes. It overwhelmed her and she wanted this…needed this…to be real. As if her desire for something more triggered a switch, her legs were suddenly on his shoulders, allowing him to sink farther inside of her. He was one with her.

"You will always be mine, Cat." Red continued to pump in and out of her with a force that took her breath away. "Touch yourself. Show me that you're mine."

Catori moved her hand in between them, gathering her cream with her middle finger and rubbing it over her sensitive clit. She cried out at the intensity of her stroke. His blue eyes remained fixated on her, although it felt as if he saw everything that she was doing. He could, couldn't he?

As if Red was surrounding her, every part of her body felt touched. Her nipples were pulled and her breasts were embraced. His lips brushed against her neck as the heat of his body blanketed her. The throbbing in her clit intensified and she pulled her hand away when it felt like his fingers had replaced hers. Over and over he stroked the engorged flesh until her breath caught in her throat and tingles rained down over her body. Her sheath contracted around his cock as he slowly continued their climb to that ever beautiful precipice.

"Kiss me," Red whispered, his voice unexpectedly near her ear. "Kiss me goodbye."

"No," Catori replied harshly, not wanting this to end. She turned her head to the side, blocking out Red's attempt at farewell. She wouldn't let him leave now. "I need more of you."

"Then don't let me go…"

Catori awoke with a start and sat straight up, looking frantically for Red. Sunlight streamed into her bedroom window, shining its unwanted rays on the tangled and twisted sheets of reality. He wasn't here. She'd have sworn differently and could still feel his keen presence. Fuck. He had felt so, so real. She placed her cool hands to her flushed face, trying to bring some sense of sanity back. So much for no nightmares, although she wasn't so sure she would qualify that dream as one.

Glancing at the clock, Catori cursed at the hour and swung her legs over the side of the bed. She didn't have time for these nightly hallucinations. All they did was make her more exhausted than she already was. She walked to the bathroom and quickly turned the knob in the shower so that the water spray came out hard enough to take a layer of skin off. She would work herself solid today and maybe join in the drills that Kane Taylor would ultimately have the team do. A difficult physical workout would exorcise the demons that haunted her at night…because he certainly hadn't been her husband.

Chapter Twelve

CATORI WALKED INTO the new location of Red Starr HRT, lifting up her sunglasses and using them to pull her hair out of her face. The place wasn't pretty, but they hadn't had the time to complete all of the offices and functional areas to her demanding standards quite yet. The large abandoned warehouse facing the pier with an attached hangar had basically started out as a tin L-shaped room of about one hundred and twenty thousand square feet.

Catori had the contractor build three separate reinforced concrete vaults to house the armory and secure the server farm and the operations room. The operations room was a multi-tiered auditorium that resembled a Star Wars command facility with all the large screen displays and banks of computers serving all the cells parsing various incoming intelligence feeds. Inside the armory there were separate areas divided by floor to ceiling cages and racks of weapons, ammo cans, and heavy-duty safes twice the size of an upright freezer. Along the right wall was the team's gear and enclosed in their own cage were large lockers containing all of their tactical and safety gear. The secure server farm required a satellite uplink and encryption gear to link the Siprnet. The entire suite was served by a four-ton air conditioning system that kept the computers comfortable at a constant sixty-five degrees and, as always, the ubiquitous two separate X08 locks with signature cards on the vault door to ensure two-person integrity.

The security system that she'd had installed would allow for keycard access to most of the training areas and the offices. The high security areas required retina scans and class three NSA approved combination locks to open and keypad sign in and out procedures once those areas were occupied each day. The entire complex, including the pier and hangar, had a twenty-four hour onsite armed security staff monitored and supervised by offsite federal contractors. It looked like security had set aside the lanyards with the small ID tags to disperse to the arriving support staff and the team when they arrived next week.

The bunkhouse was ready to receive the team and the contractors had completed the indoor small arms range. As for the offices, she'd set up six separate ones closer to the training areas for the team members. She doubted they would get much use; however, she wanted them to have an area away from the support staff to do whatever administrative work that might be required.

She placed her travel mug of coffee onto the first desk at the security checkpoint and shrugged out of her lightweight jacket, having worn it to conceal her weapon. She went around the building, turning on the lights and checking in with the master security control room, looking at the video monitors that surveyed the outer perimeter and new security fences that had been added to control sector access.

Catori been called a bitch more times in her life than she could count, but it didn't change the fact that she didn't employ very many women. She specifically wouldn't hire any in the role of tactical operations. She didn't care what the politically correct congressmen had to say about women warfighters...men acted differently in tactical situations when women got wounded and she wasn't going to introduce those added complications into her battle plan. Now a tight group of men and their raging testosterone was an entirely different story. When the men got too pent up and needed to let off a little steam, she could send them to the training areas out back to work out their issues.

Movement on one of the multitude of monitors caught Catori's attention and she smiled tiredly, having known full well that Kane Taylor wouldn't be able to keep away from seeing their new headquarters. She waited until he was right outside the front Lexan door appearing to study the textured steel before she pressed the buzzer preempting the security guard from asking who their visitor was and what he wanted. The sound of Kane's security entrance activating echoed throughout the foyer and engaged the lock on the interior door. The foyer was simple enough. It was approximately ten foot square with another door opposite the entrance. You couldn't open the second inside door until the outside entrance was closed and the lock engaged.

"Right on time, Gunny. Give me a second and I'll make my way down to the security checkpoint. We'll get you squared away."

Kane surveyed the area quietly, walking slowly around the foyer before making his way over to where security had set up the stacks of security keycards, having prepared them for their initial issue just behind the checkpoint countertop. Catori appeared around the corner from an interior hallway in denim with her favorite pair of military issued boots and a casual white cotton collared blouse.

"This is definitely a unique area to have this type of business in. I noticed several military checkpoints back up the road and along the quay." Catori led Kane down the hall after he had checked in and where security logged his retina scan, issuing him access instructions and giving him his ID, keycard, and several sets of keys. She figured she had three minutes before he asked, just about enough time to make it to her new office. "An office complex inside a giant warehouse facing a pier with an odd navy gray ship parked out back? Where the hell am I supposed to train the team? We're not SEALs."

"No, we are not," Catori said in agreement, sipping the coffee she'd made at home. It had cooled somewhat, but it was still drinkable. She'd have to utilize the new coffee pot that was situated in a common area down the hall from her office to keep her energy level up. "Which is why I've set up a three story, two thousand square foot gym area in the back of the building as well as an indoor small arms range, a weight training and cardio conditioning room, and a team briefing facility, as well as additional areas to house, feed, and equip them. The entire parameter is fenced in with a soundproof insulated covering on all exterior walls to keep prying eyes and ears out of our territory. We have around a thousand square feet high tech media room with a new generation simulator that can be programmed with various types of hostage incidents. Laser training weapons score hits on simulator projected scenario objects or personnel. The rest is your typical fitness O course, just this side of the new helo pad. As for running, that's what the beach is for. There are the beginnings of a support staff for communications, intelligence, logistics, supplies, operations, and strategic planning. That is outside of the ship's crew and flight operations and maintenance crews for the recent arrival of our new Knighthawk."

"I'm impressed," Kane said, as Catori escorted him around the extensive facility to make sure he knew where everything was. Once outside the vault door to the armory, she gave him the combo and instructed him on the retina scanning procedure. No sooner had they gotten inside than he was walking towards the weapons cages. He started with the first one, using his new set of keys to access the door leading to the racks containing the long guns, assault weapons, submachine guns, and pistols. He went down the line and surveyed all of the other cages, which ranged from heavy weapons to edged weapons and non-lethal weapon systems. Ammo, magazines and tools for working on the different systems were contained in the secondary lockers. He made sure they were secure before walking back her way. "That's one hell of an arsenal you have there."

"*We* have. Great for domestic jobs, but they won't do shit for us if we're in another country without access offshore." Catori lowered her legs and placed her travel mug down onto her desk. She reached for a keyboard and started typing, eventually pulling a materials list off of the armory's computer. "Speaking of which, you'll need to memorize this. These are our suppliers, liaisons, and contacts that I have lined up overseas in various land locked countries where we would need to utilize commercial transportation to enter. Additional files along with supplementary information are on your laptop in your office and I don't think I need to tell you that every piece of proprietary information stays within these four walls."

"What did you do? Stay here night and day since we last met?" Kane didn't peruse the information, but instead he simply closed the program and logged her out. "You look like shit."

Catori gave a half smile, already liking his candor and spunk. She shook her head as she turned to head back to her office, banking on Schultzy to have gotten her the information she'd requested. She ignored Kane's quizzical look as she started for the vault door with him in tow.

"You lasted longer than I thought you would." Catori looked around the reception area outside of her office for a place where they could keep the betting pool. "I'll bring a glass jug with me tomorrow. Never too early to start making wagers."

"I figured if you had any information on Sydney you would have told me." There wasn't a restless bone in Kane's appearance and Catori envied that. She knew she had a bad habit of chewing the inside of her cheek when she was lost in thought, so she relaxed her jaw. It was something that Red used to tease her about incessantly. She head for the coffee pot to fire them up some java. "Besides, intelligence on my sister's unit is not the reason I came to work for you."

"What?" Catori asked, hitting the brew button. She walked back his way and into her office taking a seat at her desk. "You think I'm charming?"

"There's a lot of adjectives I could think of to describe you, but charming isn't one of them."

"I'll take that as a compliment." Catori laughed at his honesty as she pulled up her email. Sure enough, though she had to enter her clearance code to access it, Schulzy had come through for her. Before pressing the envelope icon, she sat back in her chair. "I have the information you wanted. I contemplated looking at it first, but I can relate with you and what you're going through. Which is why we'll look at it together. I want your word that you'll give it six months before you even think of taking action, if any is even warranted. We may find out that it was a random attack on her unit and there was nothing to be done."

"We might," Kane conceded, but the brown in his hazel eyes practically glowed in disagreement. He nodded toward her computer as he walked around her desk and placed himself behind her. "I give you my word I'll wait six months."

"And you'll include me in on any decision you make?" Catori was looking intently at her screen and her index finger hovered over the mouse, but she waited to hear his answer. "You're my responsibility, whether this is a personal mission or not. I'll use my judgment should you need the use of the team."

"You just said this was personal." Kane leaned over her and placed his palm on her desk in his impatience. "I wouldn't jeopardize the crew."

"Within six months these men will be like your brothers." Catori turned her head and met his gaze. She wasn't willing to let this go. "Where you go, they'll go. I *will* be included on any decision you make."

"Fine, I've waited nine months. Six more won't make a difference," Kane replied curtly, nodding toward the monitor. "Click on the fucker, will you?"

She pressed the left side of the mouse. Within seconds a document opened and revealed the truth behind Sydney Taylor's death. Catori felt her stomach sink as she read line after line of what had truly transpired. Her mind whirled with the various options Kane could choose now that the actuality of his sister's mission had been laid out in front of him. This was a clusterfuck of monumental proportions and completely explained why Schultzy was sharing this information with her. He wanted her team to rescue those young natives still held captive and clean up the mess that one colonel had made with a casual directive.

"Six months?" The fury that forced those words out of Kane's mouth was vast. His restraint was remarkable. "You making me stick to that?"

"Hell, yes." Catori sat back in her chair as she digested all of the facts. This wasn't how she'd pictured Red Starr HRT starting, although the mission they were about to embark on was right up their alley. "We'll need that long to train the team in order to navigate the terrain in Nigeria. As for the colonel, it's only a matter of time before they court-martial him. Your sister's death will not be in vain. Let the justice system do its job."

"Justice has nothing to do with this," Kane explained in a voice that was devoid of emotion. "I want vengeance."

The End

Thank you for joining me on each team member's journey of
Red Starr HRT.

Hearths of Fire (Red Starr, Book 1) is available for pre-order

Moving forward with his life...

Neal Bauer tried returning home once before and he found that
some things aren't meant to be. When Red Starr HRT, a
paramilitary hostage rescue team, offered him a position that
would use his specialized skillset that had served him well in the
military—he jumped at the chance.

The past has a way of returning...

Charlotte Whitefall has made some really bad decisions in her
life...leaving Neal Bauer standing at the alter tops the list.
Growing up in Hearth, Missouri has taught her that when
someone leaves their small town, they don't return. She saved
Neal from a painful choice by moving on with her life and
raising her sister alone.

Coming home...

When a local cult invades the town of Hearth, the citizens do
their best to stay clear of the members. Everything changes
when Charlotte's little sister is drawn into their way of life. There
is only one man who has the connections to eliminate the
dangerous threat. Can Charlotte persuade Neal to come home
long enough to rescue her sister? More importantly, can she
convince him that she made a terrible mistake all those years
ago—and possibly rekindle their smoldering passion?

Books by Kennedy Layne

Surviving Ashes Series

Essential Beginnings (Surviving Ashes, Book One)
Hidden Ashes (Surviving Ashes, Book Two)

CSA Case Files Series

Captured Innocence (CSA Case Files 1)
Sinful Resurrection (CSA Case Files 2)
Renewed Faith (CSA Case Files 3)
Campaign of Desire (CSA Case Files 4)
Internal Temptation (CSA Case Files 5)
Radiant Surrender (CSA Case Files 6)

Red Starr Series

Starr's Awakening (Red Starr, The Prequel)
Hearths of Fire (Red Starr, Book One)
Targets Entangled (Red Starr, Book Two)
Igniting Passion (Red Starr, Book Three)

About the Author

First and foremost, I love life. I love that I'm a wife, mother, daughter, sister…and a writer.

I am one of the lucky women in this world who gets to do what makes them happy. As long as I have a cup of coffee (maybe two or three) and my laptop, the stories evolve themselves and I try to do them justice. I draw my inspiration from a retired Marine Master Sergeant that swept me off of my feet and has drawn me into a world that fulfills all of my deepest and darkest desires. Erotic romance, military men, intrigue, with a little bit of kinky chili pepper (his recipe), fill my head and there is nothing more satisfying than making the hero and heroine fulfill their destinies.

Thank you for having joined me on their journeys…

Email:
kennedylayneauthor@gmail.com

Facebook:
https://www.facebook.com/kennedy.layne.94

Twitter:
https://twitter.com/KennedyL_Author

Website:
www.kennedylayne.com

Newsletter:
http://www.kennedylayne.com/newsletter.html

CPSIA information can be obtained
at www.ICGtesting.com
Printed in the USA
FFOW02n1709051015
17480FF